411

4/11

African Myths and Folk Tales

Carter Godwin Woodson

DOVER PUBLICATIONS, INC.
MINEOLA, NEW YORK

DOVER CHILDREN'S THRIFT CLASSICS
GENERAL EDITOR: MARY CAROLYN WALDREP
EDITOR OF THIS VOLUME: SUZANNE E. JOHNSON

To
My Sister
Bessie Beryl Woodson

Bibliographical Note

This Dover edition, first published in 2009, is an unabridged republication of the text with a selection of illustrations from *African Myths Together with Proverbs: A Supplementary Reader Composed of Folk Tales from Various Parts of Africa, Adapted to the Use of Children in the Public Schools,* originally published by The Associated Publishers, Inc., Washington, D.C., in 1928.

Library of Congress Cataloging-in-Publication Data

Woodson, Carter Godwin, 1875–1950.
   African myths and folk tales / Carter Godwin Woodson.
      p. cm. — (Dover children's thrift classics)
   Originally published: Washington, D.C. : Associated Publishers, 1928.
   ISBN-13: 978-0-486-47734-3 (pbk.)
   ISBN-10: 0-486-47734-7 (pbk.)
   1. Tales—Africa. 2. Readers. I. Title.
   PE1127.G4W7 2010
   398.2096—dc22   2009033829

Manufactured in the United States by Courier Corporation
47734701
www.doverpublications.com

Preface

The folk tales of a people are a guide to the understanding of their past. If you want to understand people of today you must find out what they have been. If the wealth of beautiful African legends is indicative of the early civilization of that continent the natives must have reached a high level of culture. To appreciate the African, then, we must hear him speak for himself in the charming stories handed down from sire to son.

Folk tales, as a rule, deal with the terrible and formidable, telling of animal ancestors, dwarfs, and monsters; but in African stories one often discovers "tender and gracious touches." Some of these legends have a fine sense of humor. Many of them present a point of view and emphasize a moral. Taken as a whole, they show the wit, wisdom, and philosophy of the people. In this way primitive man undertook to account for the natural, moral, and spiritual world in which he moved.

Story-telling in Africa is almost an institution. Certain persons, largely old women, specialize in telling the youth interesting stories. Here and there are found professional story-tellers, those who go from place to place, devoting all of their time to this sort of occupation. They are the literary group of the tribe. They thus hand down to posterity the traditions of the fathers.

The story-teller passes as a respectable person in the community and figures especially in its social functions. In certain parts, however, story-telling is a daily performance. At the close of the day when night comes to make easy the doing of mysterious things, the group gathers around the narrator in the village street or camp to listen to a charming story.

The story is told with a wealth of descriptive detail, in a sort of dramatic, recitative chanting and crooning very much like a song. The actors in most cases are beasts; but they speak and live sometimes "as human beings in a human environment" and sometimes "as human beings in a beast environment." The narrator imitates the voice of the characters and speaks with gestures, often followed by a shriek or howl. Observers generally agree that the African story-teller does his task well.

The stories herein published are merely a few legends from different sources. Most of them may be found in varying forms in any large collection of African Folklore. These are presented here without modification of thought but in the simplest language possible to reach the minds of children of the lower grades of public schools. The glossary at the end will be helpful.

WASHINGTON, D. C.,   CARTER GODWIN WOODSON.
November, 1928.

Contents

List of Illustrations

African Myths and Folk Tales

Creation

At first there was no earth. There was Okun, the ocean, stretching over all things. Above the ocean was Olorun, the sky. Okun and Olorun contained all and possessed all things that there were.

Olorun had two sons. The elder's name was Orisha. The name of the younger son was Odudua. They were living together in the sky.

Olorun called Orisha to him. He gave him a handful of earth and a hen with five claws. Olorun said to him, "Go down and make land upon Okun, the ocean."

Orisha went. On the way he found some palm wine. He drank some of it and became drunk. Then he fell asleep.

Olorun saw this. He then called Odudua and said to him, "Thy elder brother has become drunk on his way below and has fallen asleep. Go thou, take this handful of earth and the hen with five claws and make land upon Okun."

Odudua went. He took the handful of earth. He went down and laid it on the ocean. He put the hen with five claws on it. The hen began to scratch and

1

spread the handful of earth about and forced the water aside. Much land then appeared.

The ocean grew less and less at this place and ran away through a small hole. From this small hole came holy water. This was the source of the holy river, the water of which heals and never fails.

Now Orisha was very angry because he himself had not created the earth. He and his brother fought for a long time and then both went underground and were never seen again.

Why the Sun Shines by Day and the Moon by Night

In the beginning of the world the king called the people together to be given their tasks. He sent out messengers for them. He sent the dove to call the moon, and the bat to call the sun. Each messenger was given a certain time to go and return, so that they might all arrive together.

The dove went to call the moon and brought her, and the king said, "I will give you, then, the office the sun should have had, namely, that of shining by night. When you first shine people will beat their drums and blow their trumpets; they will also bring out their fetishes for you to see them, and the fetishes of twins. These are the honors I give you."

The King tells the Sun that it is too late.

3

After giving the moon her office and honors the king waited for the bat to bring the sun; but as the bat did not come the king sent the dove to look for her and bring her.

The dove went and returned with the sun. Then the king said, "Because you have stayed so long I have given to the moon the office I meant to give to you. Now I will give you the office of showing people the way to walk about."

It was on this account that the sun hated the bat, because he loitered on the way when sent to call him, and stayed longer than the time given by the king. And very soon thereafter the sun had a chance to be even with the bat.

The bat later lived at a place with only its aged mother. Shortly after their settling there, the mother suddenly fell sick unto death. The bat called for the antelope, and said to him, "Make some medicine for my mother." The antelope looked steadily at her to see what her disease was. Then he told the bat, "There is no one who has the medicine that will cure your mother, except the sun." After saying this, the antelope returned home.

On another day, early in the morning, the bat arose to go to call the sun. He did

The Bat

not start until about seven o'clock. He met the sun on the road around eleven o'clock. And he said to the sun, "My journey was on the way to see you."

The sun replied, "If you have a word to say, speak!"

So the bat requested, "Come! make some medicine for my mother. She is sick."

But the sun replied, "I can't go to make medicine unless you meet me in my house; not here on the road. Go back; and come to me at my house tomorrow."

So the bat went back home. And the day darkened, night came, and all went to sleep.

At six o'clock the next day, the bat started out to call the sun. About nine o'clock, he met the sun on the path; and he told the sun what he had come for. But the sun said to him, "Whenever I leave my house, I do not go back, but I keep on to the end of my journey. Go back, for another day." The bat returned home again.

He made other journeys in order to see the sun at his house, five successive days; but every day he was late, and met the sun already on the way of his own journey for his own business.

Finally, on the seventh day, the bat's mother died. Then the bat, in his grief said, "It is the sun who has killed my mother! Had he made some medicine for her, she would have become well."

Very many people from afar came together that day at the mourning for the dead. The funeral was

Quadrupeds at the funeral of the Bat

held from six o'clock in the morning until eleven o'clock of the next day. At that hour, the bat announced, "Let her be taken to the grave." He called other beasts to go into the house together with him, in order to carry out the corpse. They took up the body, and carried it on the way to the grave.

On their arrival at the grave, these beasts said to the bat, "We have a rule that, before we bury a person, we must first look upon the face to see who it is." They then opened the coffin.

When they had looked on the face, they said, "No! we can't bury this person; for, it is not our relative, it does not belong to us beasts. This person looks like us because he has teeth. And it also has a head like us. But, that it has wings, makes it look like a bird. It is a bird. Call for the birds! We shall leave." So they departed.

Then the bat called the birds to come. They came, big and little; pelicans, eagles, herons and all the others. When they all had come together, they said to the bat, "Show us the dead body."

He said to them, "Here it is! Come! look upon it!"

They looked at it very carefully. Then they said, "Yes! it resembles us; for, it has wings as we have. But, about the teeth, no! We birds, none of us, have any teeth. This person does not resemble us with those teeth. It does not belong to us."

And all the birds stepped aside.

During the time that the talking had been going on, ants had come and laid hold of the body, and could not be driven away. Then one of the birds said to the bat, "I told you, you ought not to delay the burial, for many things might happen."

Birds at the funeral of the Bat

And all the birds and beasts went away.

The bat, left alone, said to himself, "The wicked sun alone is to blame for all of my troubles. If he had made some medicine, my mother would not be dead. So, I, the bat, and the sun shall not look on each other again. We shall have no friendship. When he appears, I shall hide myself. I won't meet him or look at him."

"And," he added, "I shall mourn for my mother always. I will make no visits. I will walk about only at night, not in the daytime, lest I meet the sun or other people."

How Animals Came into the World

Famine in a strange land had lasted nearly three years. In that land lived a man called Kweku Tsin. As he was very hungry, Kweku Tsin looked daily in the forest to find food.

One day he happened to see three palm kernels on the ground. He picked up two stones with which to crack them. The first nut, however, slipped when he hit it, and rolled into a hole behind him. The same thing happened to the second and to the third. This annoyed Kweku very much, and he determined to go down the hole to seek his lost palm kernels.

When he reached the hole, however, he was surprised to learn that it was the entrance to a town, of which he had never before even heard. When he entered it he found deathlike silence everywhere. He cried aloud, "Is there nobody in this town?" And soon he heard a voice in reply. He went in that direction and found an old woman creeping along one of the streets. She stopped and asked why he had come there, and he quickly told her.

The old woman was very kind and sympathetic; and promised to help him, if he would do as she

told him. "Go into the garden and listen attentively," said she. "You will hear the yams speak.
Pass by any yam that says, 'Dig me out, dig me
out!' But take the one that says, 'Do not dig me
out!' Then bring it to me."

When he brought the yam, she directed him to
remove the peel from it and throw the yam away.
He was then to boil the rind, and, while boiling, it
would become a yam.

*The Old Woman
creeping along.*

It turned out as she said,
and they sat down to eat
some of it. Before taking
the meal the old woman requested Kweku not to look
at her while she ate. He was
very polite and obedient, and
kept his head turned.

In the evening the old
woman sent him into the garden to get one of the drums
which were there. She told
him, "If you come to a drum
which says, 'Ding-ding,' when
you touch it, take it. But be
very careful not to take one
which says, 'Dong-dong.' "

He carefully obeyed her or-
ders. When he showed her the drum, she looked
pleased and told him, to his great delight, that he
had only to beat it if at any time he were hungry.

That would bring him food in plenty. He thanked the old woman very much and went home.

As soon as Kweku Tsin reached his own home, he called his household together, and then beat the drum. All at once, food of every kind came before them, and they all ate and ate until they wanted no more.

The next day Kweku Tsin called all the people of the village together in the public square, and then beat the drum once more. In this way every family received sufficient food for its wants, and all thanked Kweku Tsin very much for thus giving them what they so much needed.

The Magic Drum

Anansi, Kweku's father, however, was jealous of his son who was able to feed the whole village. Anansi thought he, too, should have a magic drum. The people then would be grateful to him instead of to his son.

He asked the young man, therefore, where he had found the wonderful drum. His son at first refused to tell him, but Anansi gave him no peace until he had learned the whole story.

He then immediately went off toward the hole leading to the town. He carried with him an old nut which he pretended to crack; but he threw it into the hole, and jumped in after it, and hurried along to the silent village.

When he came to the first house, he cried, "Is there no one in this town?" The old woman answered as she did when the son came, and Anansi entered her home.

He was in too much haste to be polite and spoke to her very rudely, saying, "Hurry up, old woman, and get me something to eat."

The woman politely asked him to go into the garden and choose the yam which should say, "Do not dig me out."

Anansi laughed at her and said, "You surely take me for a dunce. If the yam does not want me to dig it out I would be very silly to do so. I shall take the one which wants to be dug out." And so he did.

When he brought the yam to the old woman she told him, as she had told his son, to throw away the inside and boil the rind; but he refused to obey.

"Who ever heard of such a silly thing as throwing away the inside and boiling the peel," said Anansi.

He did so, and the yam turned into stones. He then saw that it was better to do as he had been told, and boil the rind. While boiling the rind turned into yam.

Anansi then turned in anger to the old woman and said, "You are a witch."

The Garden

She took no notice of his words, but went on putting the food on the table. She placed his dinner on a small table, lower than her own, saying, "You must not look at me while I eat."

He rudely replied, "Indeed, I will look at you if I choose. And I will have my dinner at your table, not at that small one."

Again she said nothing, but she did not touch her dinner. Anansi ate his own and hers too.

Animals on Earth

When he had finished eating she said, "Now go into the garden and choose a drum. Do not take the one which sounds 'Dong-dong'; take the one which says 'Ding-ding.'"

Anansi then said, "Do you think I will take your advice, you witch? No. I will choose the drum which says 'Dong-dong.' You are just trying to play a trick on me."

He did as he wished. Having secured the drum he marched off without so much as thanking the old woman.

No sooner had he reached home, than he thought to show off his new power to the villagers. He called all to the public square, and told them to bring dishes and trays, as he was going to supply them with food. The people in great joy rushed to the spot. Anansi took his position in the midst of them, and began to beat his drum. To his surprise and horror, instead of the abundance of foodstuffs which Kweku had summoned, Anansi saw, rushing toward him, beasts and serpents of all kinds. Such things had never been seen on the earth before.

All the people except Anansi fled in every direction. He was too frightened to move and was quickly devoured by the animals. Thus he had been speedily punished for his disobedience.

Fortunately, Kweku, with his mother and sisters, had been at the outer edge of the crowd, and they easily escaped into shelter. The animals then went in all directions and ever since they have roamed wild in the forests.

————————

A man with wisdom is better off than a stupid man with any amount of charm and superstition.

No man puts new cloth into an old garment.

The Origin of Lake Tanganyika

Long, long ago, in the region where you see the lake, there was a wide plain where lived many tribes who had large herds of oxen and goats.

In this plain was a very large village. As was the custom in those days, all the houses of this village were surrounded by tall hedges with stalls where people drove in their cattle for the night to keep them from wild beasts and robbers.

In one of these enclosures there lived with his wife a man who owned a deep spring from which a little stream came.

This spring, strange to say, contained many kinds of fishes which the man and his wife used for food; but this large supply of food was a secret. No one outside the family knew it.

A story handed down from father to son said that the day when the secret should be told by one of them to strangers, the family would be ruined and destroyed. It was very necessary, then, to keep this secret.

By and by there came into this family a pretty daughter. She grew to be a woman and many young men from around came to admire her.

It happened, unknown to the father and mother, that the daughter loved one of these men, and her love for him increased. One day she secretly brought the young man some fish from the wonderful spring. The flesh was so good and of such a fine flavor that her lover wanted to know whence it came. The daughter kept silent for a long time through fear of what might happen if she told the secret. Finally she promised to tell it. Her love for the young man was so great as to make her believe that she must do whatever he asked of her.

One day the mother and father had to make a journey; before starting they strictly cautioned their daughter to keep the secret about the wonderful spring, to admit no stranger into the home, and not to gossip with the neighbors.

The daughter promised; but as soon as the mother and father had started she went hurriedly to find her lover.

"Come," said she, "you are going to learn now where the fish comes from."

Her lover went with her. He entered the house, where the daughter gave him palm wine, bananas, sorghum porridge, palm oil, seasoned with pepper, and a quantity of fish.

When he had finished the meal, the man said, "Show me where you catch the fish."

She replied, "Yes, but it is a secret which, if told, will cause great misfortunes."

"Fear not," said her lover.

They rose. She led him within the enclosure and showed him what seemed to be a little pool, round in shape and full of clear water, which bubbled out of the ground.

"Look," said she, "there is the wonderful spring, and there are the delicious fish."

The young man had never seen anything like it, for there was no river nearby. A fish came near him, and he stretched out his hand to catch it. Alas! that was the end of everything!

The muzimu (spirit) was enraged. The earth split asunder; the plain sank so deep that the longest plummet cannot go to the bottom of it; the spring overflowed and filled the great chasm which had appeared in the earth.

And now what do you see at the spot? Tanganyika.

The Beginning of Death

When Kintu first came to the earth he found there was no food at all. He brought with him one cow and had only its milk for his food. In the course of time a woman named Nambi came with her brother to the earth and saw Kintu. The woman fell in love with him. She wished to be married to him, and told him so. But she had to return with her brother to her people and her father, Gulu, who was king of the sky.

Nambi's relatives objected to the marriage because they said that the man did not know of any food except that which the cow gave, and they did not like him. Gulu their father, however, said they had better test Kintu before he agreed to the marriage. He then sent his son to take Kintu's cow. For a time Kintu was at a loss what to eat, but he learned to eat herbs.

Nambi happened to see the cow and knew it. She complained that her brothers wished to kill the man she loved. She then went to the earth and told Kintu where his cow was, and invited him to return with her to take it away. Kintu consented and went.

19

When Nambi's brothers saw Kintu with their sister, they told their father. He ordered them to build a house for Kintu and said they were to put him to another test.

An enormous meal was cooked, enough food for a hundred people, and brought to Kintu. He was told that unless he ate it all he would be killed as a thief. If he failed to eat it, they said, this would be proof that he was not the great Kintu. He was then shut up in a house and left.

After he had eaten and drunk as much as he wished, he did not know what to do with the rest of the food. Fortunately he discovered a deep hole in the floor of the house. He turned all the food and beer into it and covered it over so that no one could detect the place. He then called the people outside.

The sons of Gulu came in, but would not believe he had eaten all the food. They, therefore, searched the house, but failed to find anything.

They then went to their father and told him that Kintu had eaten all the food. He would not believe the story, and said Kintu must be further tested. A copper ax was sent by Gulu, who said to Kintu, "Go and cut me firewood from the rock, because I do not use ordinary firewood."

When Kintu went with the ax he said to himself, "What am I to do? If I strike the rock, the ax will only turn its edge or rebound." However, after he had looked at the rock he found there were cracks in it. He broke off pieces, then, and returned with them to Gulu, who was surprised to get them.

Still he said Kintu must be further tried before they gave their consent to the marriage. Kintu was next sent to get water and was told he must bring dew only, because Gulu did not drink water from wells. Kintu took the water-pot and went off to a field where he put the pot down and began to ponder what he was to do to collect the dew. He was sorely puzzled; but, upon returning to the pot, he found it full of water, and he carried it back to Gulu.

Gulu was most surprised and said, "This man is a wonderful being; he shall have his cow back and marry my daughter."

Kintu was told he was to pick his cow from the herd and take it. This was a more difficult task than the others. Since there were so many cows like his own he feared he would take the wrong one.

While he was thus puzzled a large bee came and said, "Take the one upon whose horns I shall alight; it is yours."

The next morning he went to the appointed place and stood and watched the bee which was resting on a tree near him. A large herd of cows was brought before him, and he pretended to look for his cow; but in reality he watched the bee, which did not move.

After a time Kintu said, "My cow is not there."

A second herd was brought, and again he said, "My cow is not there."

A third much larger herd was brought, and the bee flew at once and rested upon a cow which was a very large one, and Kintu said, "That is my cow."

The bee then flew to another cow, and Kintu said, "That is one of the calves from my cow," and so on to a second and third which he claimed as the calves that had been born during the cow's stay with Gulu.

Gulu was delighted with Kintu and said, "You are truly Kintu; take your cows: no one can deceive or rob you; you are too smart for that."

African Cattle

He called Nambi and said to Kintu, "Take my daughter who loves you, marry her and go back to your home."

Gulu further said, "You must hurry away and go back before Death (Walumbe) comes, because he will want to go with you and you must not take him; he will only cause you trouble and unhappiness."

Nambi agreed to what her father said and went to pack up her things. Kintu and Nambi then took leave of Gulu, who said, "Be sure if you have forgotten anything not to come back, because Death will want to go with you and you must go without him."

They started off home, taking with them, besides Nambi's things and the cows, a goat, a sheep, a fowl, and a plantain tree. On the way Nambi looked into her basket and found out that she had forgotten the grain for the fowl, and said to Kintu, "I must go back for the grain for the fowl, or it will die."

Kintu told her not to go back, but in vain. She said, "I will hurry back and get in without any one seeing me."

He said, "Your brother Death will be on the watch and see you."

She would not listen to her husband, but went back and said to her father, "I have forgotten the grain for the fowl, and I am come to take it from the doorway where I put it."

He replied, "Did I not tell you that you were not to return if you forgot anything, because your brother Death would see you and want to go with you? Now he will accompany you."

She tried to steal away without Death, but he followed her.

When she returned to Kintu, he was angry at seeing Death, and said, "Why have you brought your brother with you? Who can live with him?"

Nambi was sorry; so Kintu said, "Let us go on and see what will happen."

When they reached the earth Nambi planted her garden, and the plantains grew rapidly, and she soon had a large plantain grove. They lived happily for some time and had a number of children, until one day Death asked Kintu to send one of his children to be his cook.

Kintu replied, "If Gulu comes and asks me for one of my children, what am I to say to him? Shall I tell him that I have given her to be your cook?"

Death was silent and went away, but he again asked for a child to be his cook, and again Kintu refused to send one of his daughters to serve Death in this or any other way.

Death

Death then said, "I will kill them."

Kintu, who did not know what he meant, asked, "What is it you will do?"

In a short time, however, one of the children fell ill and died, and from that time they began to die at intervals. Kintu returned to Gulu and told him about the passing of the children, and accused Death of being the cause.

Gulu replied, "Did I not tell you when you were going away to go at once with your wife and not to return if you had forgotten anything, but you allowed Nambi to return for the grain? Now you have Death living with you. Had you obeyed me you would have been free from him and not lost any of your children."

After some further entreaty, Gulu sent Kaikuzi, the brother of Death, to assist Nambi, and to prevent Death from killing the children.

Kaikuzi went to the earth with Kintu and was met by Nambi, who told him her pitiful story. He said he would call Death and ask him not to kill the children.

When Death came to greet his brother they had quite a pleasant meeting, and Kaikuzi told him he had come to take him back, because their father wanted him.

Death said, "Let us take our sister, too"; but Kaikuzi said he was not sent to take her, because she was married and had to stay with her husband.

Death refused to go without his sister, and Kaikuzi was angry with him and ordered him to do as he was told. Death, however, escaped from Kaikuzi's grip and fled away into the earth.

For a long time there was strife between the two brothers. Kaikuzi tried in every possible way to catch his brother Death, who always escaped. At last Kaikuzi told the people to remain in their houses for several days and not let any of the animals out, and he would have a final hunt for Death. He further told them that if they saw Death they must not call out nor raise the usual cry.

The instructions were followed for two or three days, and Kaikuzi got his brother to come out of the earth and was about to capture him, when some children took their goats to the pasture and saw Death and called out. Kaikuzi rushed to the spot and asked why they called, and was told they had seen Death. He was angry, because Death had gone into the earth again.

He went to Kintu, then, and told him he was tired of hunting Death and wanted to return home. He also complained that the children had frightened Death into the earth again. Kintu thanked Kaikuzi for his help and said he feared nothing more could be done, and hoped Death would not kill all the people.

From that time Death has lived upon the earth and killed people whenever he could, and then escaped into the earth.

Regret causes an aching which is worse than pain.

After a foolish action comes remorse.

Remorse weeps tears of blood and gives the echo of what is lost forever.

Why Children Belong to the Mother

There was once an animal called Ejimm, which had two sons named Obegud and Igwe. They lived in the forest, near the home of a poor man and wife who had twelve children.

One day these parents left their children at home and went to their farm. While they were away and the children were singing and playing together the wicked beast Ejimm heard their voices.

She sent her son Obegud to their home to say that he had something to sell. The beast did so, and the children asked him to show his wares.

As soon as he had succeeded so far in attracting their attention, he went back singing a song to let Ejimm know that all was well. Ejimm then rushed to the home, and stood outside of the gate—a fearful sight! Then she thrust out her long sharp claws, seized a child, and carried it off to her den in the woods.

On their return from work on the plantation, the parents missed one of their children. They heard from the others that a monster with a very long mouth had killed him and carried him off.

The Father running from the Beast

Long they wept for their lost child, and when the time came to go to the farm next day, the father bade his wife go alone while he waited at home to catch Ejimm. At first the woman would not go, but after a while her husband persuaded her, so she left him and went on.

At noon the beast sent out her other son Igwe, telling him to say what his brother Obegud had said the day before. He did so, and again the children asked him to bring out his wares. He then ran homeward, singing as he went another song as a sign to Ejimm that all was well.

When Ejimm heard this she again came out to take one of the children. She came to the gate as before. The man was well armed, but at the horrible sight of the beast he lost his courage. He ran for his life through the forest. He left his children helpless before the greedy monster. Ejimm, then, seized another child and carried it off to make of it a great feast.

When the mother returned and learned that a second child had been taken, she was heartbroken. With her eyes filled with tears she turned fiercely on her husband, and asked why he had not saved his child.

To cover up his cowardice, he told her that he had become suddenly sick, and had had to leave the infants for a while, and during his short absence the monster had come and had taken another.

The children, however, all cried out, "No, Mother. Father fled in terror at the sight of the animal, and left us to face the danger alone."

The mother was angry at him for his cowardly act, and drove him away. He did not need to be told a second time. He went out and hid himself in the woods nearby.

He ran back to his hiding place.

The mother said she would risk her life to save her children. She got a very sharp sword, and waited for the beast, which came again as before, and thrust her head through the gate to seize a child. Then the woman took courage, faced the danger, and killed the beast. The children gave loud shouts of joy.

The father who had heard all of this came from his hiding place in the hope that all danger was then over. Obegud and Igwe, the two sons of Ejimm, however, had heard the noise of the struggle, and now rushed out to the aid of their mother. When the man saw these other two monsters he ran back to his hiding place, but the woman held her position and was not afraid. She saved her children and killed the beasts.

When the mother had finished the fight with the beasts, out came the worthless husband from his hiding place, and asked for a knife, that he might divide the flesh of the beasts between himself and his wife. The best of the flesh he kept for his share, and gave the heads only to the woman who had saved the children and had slain the beasts.

To this the mother of the children refused to agree. She called upon Master Obassi to decide between her husband and herself. To whom did the flesh of the beasts belong?

Obassi heard her cry, and sent a messenger to bring them before him. When they arrived, the wife stood forth, bowed and said:

"After promising to fight Ejimm and protect our children, my husband ran away, and left them for the monster to kill. I am the one who stood forth fighting, and slew, not only the beast but also her two young. Yet my husband desires to give me only the heads of all these animals. I come, then, to claim my right before our Master."

Obassi then asked the husband what he had to say in defense of taking such a large share; but he could not dispute what his wife had said.

It was clear to Obassi that the wife had the brave heart to defend her children when their father had fled in fear. Obassi scolded the husband for deserting his children. He, then, gave order that from thenceforward no man should claim any property which his wife had risked her life to get.

Obassi also said, that, should the wife choose to take the other ten children away from her husband, she should be permitted to do so; for she had suffered much for their sakes.

A woman is sure to risk her life for her children, though there are but few men who will do so.

It is because of this decision that when a woman leaves her husband and returns to her parents, she may be forced to give up all gifts received from him, but not her children, nor any other thing for which she may have risked her life.

Hold a true friend with both hands.

A counsellor who understands proverbs soon sets difficult matters aright.

Nobody is twice a dunce.

Remember that all flowers of a tree do not bear fruit.

The Ingrate

A very poor hunter was one day walking through the woods in search of food. He came to a deep hole, and found there a leopard, a serpent, a rat, and a man. They had all fallen into the trap and could not escape. When they saw the hunter, they begged him to get them out of the trap.

At first the hunter did not wish to help out any but the man. The leopard, he said, had often taken his cattle and had eaten them. The serpent very frequently bit men to death. The rat was no good to any one. He saw no wisdom, then, in setting them free.

However, these animals begged so hard for their lives that at last he helped them out of the pit. All in turn, except the man, promised to reward the hunter for his kindness. The man said he was very poor, and the kind-hearted hunter took him home and cared for him.

A short time thereafter the serpent came to the hunter and gave him a very effective cure for snake-poison.

"Keep it carefully," said the serpent. "You will find it very useful one day. When you are using it, be sure to ask for the blood of a traitor to mix with it."

The hunter thanked the serpent very much; he took great care of the powder and always carried it about with him.

The leopard also showed his gratitude by catching game for the hunter and bringing him food of various kinds for many weeks.

Finally, one day the rat came to the hunter and gave him a large bundle.

"These," said he, "are some native cloths, gold dust, and ivory. They will make you rich."

The hunter thanked the rat and took the bundle into his home.

After this the hunter was able to live in much ease and comfort. He built himself a fine new house and put in it everything needful. The man whom he had taken out of the pit still lived with him and enjoyed everything the hunter had in his home.

This man, however, was very covetous. He did not want to see the hunter have such a fortune, and only waited the chance to do him some harm. Such a chance soon came.

Word was given throughout the country that some robbers had broken into the king's palace and had stolen his jewels and many other treasures. The ungrateful man rushed at once to the king and asked what would be the reward for telling him the name of the thief. The king told him it would be half of the things which had been stolen. The ungrateful man then falsely said that his friend was the thief, although he well knew that the hunter had not stolen anything.

The honest hunter was rushed into prison. He was then brought into court and asked to explain how he had become so rich. He truthfully told them how he got his wealth, but no one believed him. He was therefore condemned to die the next day.

Next morning, while the officers of the court were preparing to take his life, word was brought to the prison that the king's eldest son had been bitten by a serpent and was about to die. Any one who could cure him was begged to come and do so.

The hunter at once thought of the powder which his serpent friend had given him, and asked the officers to let him use it in curing the king's son. At first they would not let him try, but finally consented. The king asked him if there were anything he needed for the powder and he replied, "A traitor's blood to mix it with."

The king at once pointed out the wicked fellow who had falsely accused the hunter and said, "There stands the worst traitor, for he tried to sell the head of the friend who saved his life."

The man was at once beheaded and the powder was mixed as the serpent had commanded. As soon as it was applied to the wound of the prince the young man became well. In the midst of great joy, the king gave the hunter many honors and sent him home happy.

The Jealousy of the Blind Man

Two brown men were blind, and they both took a walk to find some one or something to help their condition. The one in front found a little horn and he blew it. As soon as he blew it his eyes were opened and he could see. How happy he was to be able to see again the beautiful world!

He said to the other blind man, "I found a little horn and blew it, and now I can see."

He gave it to the blind man to blow, and he blew it and he could see also. He was both happy and thankful that he also could see.

But as soon as the second man obtained his sight he threw away the horn.

The man who found it said, "Where is my horn?"

The other replied, "I threw it away."

"Give me my horn," replied the first man. The second man went and found the horn.

"Here is your horn," said the second man as he handed it to the first man.

The first man was jealous because the second man could see, and he thought by blowing again he could be made to see much better than the other man. So he blew his horn again and became blind.

As soon as he saw that he was blind, he handed the horn to the second man, saying, "I have fixed my eyes better than yours; you fix yours now."

The second man replied, "I do not wish to blow again: I am satisfied with my sight. Before, I could not see at all and I am thankful for the sight I have obtained; you keep the horn."

The first man became enraged and demanded that the second man must blow or fight.

"I cannot blow, so we must fight, then," said the second man, whereupon he ran away and left the jealous man helpless and blind.

His ingratitude and jealousy had caused him to lose his sight. He was not thankful for the blessing which he had received. He wanted more than his companion had received.

"Jealousy is self-love." One should not love himself. He should love others. In the end jealousy harms the jealous man himself. Africans, therefore, warn against jealousy and fear it as a green-eyed monster.

The Race for a Wife

A man had a daughter who liked all the creatures of the forest. Each of them was trying to secure the daughter for his wife, and the daughter was unable to decide which one she wanted.

They all went to the father for his consent. Each one explained to the father how he was the best man for his daughter. Everybody was singing his own praise.

The father told them to wait, that he would place his daughter in the old field, and that the one who reached there first should have his daughter.

They all agreed to enter the race. Each one began to plan how he could do his best to reach her first.

When they all assembled the fox said, "We must catch the deer and tie him, or he will win the race, as he can run much faster than any of us."

So they all combined and tied the deer and started on the race.

The Spider unties the Deer.

After they had gotten on the way the spider came along and saw the deer tied fast.

The spider asked, "What are you doing tied?"

The deer told him how all the animals had combined to tie him in order to keep him from winning the race and securing the daughter of the old man.

The spider then said, "If I let you loose what will you pay me?"

The deer said that if he won the race he would give the spider their first daughter for a wife. The spider then untied him and jumped on the deer's horn.

The deer, then, ran and ran and finally passed all the other animals. When he got in the old field near the old man's house the spider jumped down and ran to the girl before the deer could reach her.

The deer said that the girl belonged to him because he had brought the spider and without him the spider could not have got there at all. The spider said she was his because he was the first to go up to the girl and claim her, and if he had not untied the deer he could not have entered the race at all, so they submitted the matter to the judge, who decided that the spider won the race and therefore was entitled to the old man's daughter.

The Deer and the Snail

The deer said to the snail, "I can run faster than you."

"You cannot," replied the snail. "You cannot tell what one can do by looking at him."

"I will bet you that I can," said the deer.

"What will you bet?" asked the snail without any fear. He had a plan for winning the race.

"Let us see who can run first to a town across the plain," said the deer, "and the one who loses, he and all his people shall be servants to the other and his people."

"I agree," replied the snail. "Let it be so."

The snail went and told all his people about the race. He stationed them at a certain distance apart

along the way they were to run, and had one snail stop in the town to which the race was to be made.

The snail knew he could not run, and so he sought the help of all his people. But the

40

deer felt so confident of winning the race against the snail that he did not tell any of his people.

The Deer and the Snail in a race.

Having gotten all his people arranged, the snail told the deer that he was ready for the race. Off they went.

About a mile away the deer came to a river, and when he got there the snail's brother cried out, "I am here too and you must carry me across."

"All right," said the deer, "but I have not started to run yet."

The deer ran to the next river and a snail cried out again," I am here and you must carry me across."

The deer carried him across, and said, "I see I must run to beat you."

So the deer began to do his best in running.

When he got to the next river the snail cried out, "I have been here a long time, deer. What have you been doing so long? You must carry me across too."

The deer carried him across, and started on his last run to the town.

The deer ran and he ran; at length all exhausted he reached the town, and as soon as he entered he saw the snail. The deer hallooed and ran away without waiting for the judge to decide the race. And ever since that day when the deer sees the snail he is afraid and he runs.

Ohia and His Sorrows

There once lived upon the earth a poor man called Ohia. He had a wife named Awirehu. This unlucky couple had had one misfortune after another. No matter what they took in hand trouble seemed to lie in wait for them. Everything they did met with failure. They became so poor that at last they could scarcely obtain a cloth with which to cover their nakedness.

Finally, Ohia thought of doing a thing at which many of his village had succeeded. He went to a wealthy farmer near by and offered to cut his palm trees to make wine from the sap.

Ohia planned to catch the sap in pots. When this would be ready for the market, his wife would sell it. The money received for it would then be divided equally among the three.

When this plan was laid before the farmer, he readily agreed to it. Not only so, but he gave Ohia some earthen pots in which to collect the sap, for the poor man was not able to buy anything.

In great delight Ohia and his wife went to work. They cut down the trees and prepared them. They set the pots underneath to catch the sap. Before daybreak on market day, Ohia went out, with a lighted torch, to collect the wine and prepare it that his wife might take it into the town.

To his great surprise, on arriving at the trees, instead of finding his earthen pots filled with the sweet sap, he saw them lying broken in pieces on the ground.

Misfortune had overtaken him again. He secured new pots and found them broken the same way the second day. He had the same experience again but he got other pots only to find them gone in the same way.

This was sad but he took courage and set his pots in order for the last time. When night came, he stayed among the trees to watch for the thief. Midnight passed and nothing happened, but about two o'clock in the morning a dark form passed him on the way to the nearest palm tree. A moment after he heard the sound of a breaking pot. He crept up to the form and found out that the thief was a bush deer. It carried on its head a jar into which it was pouring the wine from the pots. Ohia tried to seize the bush deer, but it was too quick for him and escaped, dropping his pot on the ground.

The deer was so swift that it outran Ohia, but he followed and followed until he came to the top of a hill in the midst of a great gathering of animals of which the lion was king. Ohia had run into this group of animals so suddenly that he knew not what to do or say. King Lion ordered that Ohia be brought before him to be punished for disturbing the peace of the animals.

Ohia begged for a chance to explain the affair. King Lion agreed to listen to him. Ohia then told the story of his poverty and how he finally found out how to make palm wine which the bush deer was stealing.

The animals were pleased with this story and agreed that the deer was guilty. The deer was punished. King Lion, each morning, it was learned, had given the deer a large sum of money to purchase palm wine for them. The deer had stolen the wine and kept the money for some other purpose.

To make up for Ohia's losses, King Lion offered him, as a gift, the power of understanding the language of all animals. This, said he, would speedily make Ohia a rich man. But he gave him this secret on the condition that Ohia must never—on pain of instant death—let any one know about his wonderful power.

The poor man, much delighted, started for home. When he arrived he at once began to make palm wine and had no more of such troubles with his pots. He and his wife were, therefore, happy.

One morning, while he was bathing in a pool near his home, he heard a hen and her chickens talking together in the garden. He listened, and heard a chicken tell the mother hen about three jars of gold buried in Ohia's garden. The hen told the chicken to be careful, that her master might not see her scratching near the gold, and thereby discover it.

Ohia pretended not to notice what they were saying, and went away. As soon as the mother hen and her brood had gone, however, he came back and began to dig in that part of the garden.

To his great delight he soon found three jars of gold. In them was enough money to keep him in comfort all his life. He was careful, however, not to mention his treasure to any one but his wife. He hid it safely inside his home.

Soon Ohia and Awirehu had become one of the richest couples in the country. They owned a large amount of property. Ohia thought he could afford now to keep a head housekeeper to relieve his wife; so he hired one.

Unfortunately, the new woman did not at all resemble Awirehu, who had always been a good, kind, and honest wife. The new woman was very jealous and selfish. In addition to this, she was lame and always thought that people were making fun of her.

She had the idea that Ohia and Awirehu—when together—were accustomed to laugh at her. Nothing was further from their thoughts, but she refused to believe it. Whenever she saw them together she would creep up and listen outside the door to hear what they were saying. Of course, she never heard them say anything about her.

At last, one evening, Ohia and Awirehu had gone to bed. His wife was fast asleep when he heard a conversation which amused him very much. Two little mice were arranging to go to the larder to take some food as soon as their master—who was watching them—fell asleep.

Ohia, taking this to be a good joke, laughed outright. The lame woman heard him, rushed into the room, and accused him of making fun of her again to Awirehu.

The astonished man, of course, denied this, but she said again and again that it was true. The jealous woman said that, if he were laughing at an innocent joke, he would at once tell it to her. But Ohia could not do this without breaking his promise to King Lion.

His refusal, however, made the woman more suspicious, and she did not rest till she had told the chief about the whole matter. As he was a friend of Ohia, the chief tried to persuade him to tell what the joke was and set the matter at rest. Ohia would not agree to do such a thing. The troublesome woman gave the chief no peace till he called Ohia to answer her charge before the assembly in the public square.

As there was, then, no other way out of the difficulty, Ohia prepared for death. He first invited all his friends and relatives to a great feast, and bade them farewell. Then he put his affairs in order. He gave all his gold to the faithful Awirehu, and his property to his son and servants. When he had finished, he went to the public square where the people of the village were assembled.

He first took leave of the chief, and then began his story. He spoke of his many misfortunes, of his pursuit of the deer, of the secret which was given him, and of his promise to King Lion. Finally, he explained the cause of his laughter which had annoyed the lame woman. While thus speaking he fell dead, as King Lion had warned him.

He was buried amid great sorrow; for none knew him but to love and respect him. The jealous woman who had caused Ohia's death was seized and burnt as a witch. Her ashes were then scattered to the four winds of heaven, and it is because of this fact that jealousy and selfishness are so widespread throughout the world, where before they could scarcely be found.

It is better to be poor and live long than rich and die young.

A man may be born to wealth, but wisdom comes only with length of days.

Why Some Women Never Eat Mutton

Once upon a time there was a man named Kiwobe who had a sheep and an only son named Kakange. One day Kiwobe went out to visit a friend, and the sheep said to the boy Kakange, "Kiwobe said when you saw the sun shining you were to take me out to the pasture; what are you doing? Are you waiting until it is evening to take me out?"

When the man returned home, his son told him what the sheep had said.

Kiwobe said, "My child, why do you tell a falsehood? Can a sheep talk like a man?"

The boy said, "If you think I am telling you a falsehood, pretend you are going away, and after going a little distance, turn back and hide near the door and listen, and you will hear it speak."

Kiwobe did as the boy had suggested; he hid near the house, and after a short time the sheep called to the boy and asked, "What did Kiwobe tell you?"

The boy replied, "He said, 'When you see the sun shining untie the sheep, and take it out to the pasture.'"

The sheep said, "Well, what do you see now?"

When Kiwobe heard it, he went and told his companions, saying he did not know what to do because his sheep had spoken like a man to his son.

His companions told him to cut a palm pole, bring it, and drop it upon the sheep and kill it. Kiwobe brought the pole and dropped it by the sheep; the sheep, however, sprang aside and escaped, and said to Kiwobe, "Do you want to kill me? I will not blame you this time, because you are tired."

When Kiwobe saw he had failed to kill the sheep he left the place secretly, and went to live elsewhere, leaving the sheep tied in the house; he had also forgotten to take with him his ax-handle. The sheep took the ax-handle and followed the man along the road and found him at a dance.

The sheep said to the people dancing, "What kind of a dance is this?" and at once began to dance and sing: "This is coming, yes, but not arrived; this is coming, yes, but not arrived."

As the sheep was dancing it saw its master Kiwobe, and went to him and said, "My brother, why did you leave me in the house? You also left your ax-handle which I have brought."

All the people at the dance were greatly surprised to hear the sheep speak, but Kiwobe fled away and the sheep ran after him, and they both arrived together at the house. Kiwobe then agreed with his wife that she should kill the sheep when he went away for a walk.

The sheep, however, heard the man tell his wife to kill it, and when Kiwobe had gone the sheep caught the woman and killed her. It then cut the woman up and cooked her, and took her clothes and put them on.

When Kiwobe returned he asked his wife if she had killed the sheep, and it replied, "Yes; and I am cooking it now."

Kiwobe said, "Dish up the food," and the sheep did so, and the man sat down to eat his meal.

When Kiwobe was eating his son came up and said to him, "Sir, that which brings your food is the sheep, it has killed your wife and cooked her."

When Kiwobe heard this he rose up, and got his spear to kill the sheep, but it fled away and escaped during the night.

This is the reason why some women never eat mutton.

The Fairy Wife

There were two sons of one mother, one named Mavungu, and the other Luemba. Luemba was a fine child, and grew up to be a handsome man. Mavungu was puny and miserable-looking, and as he came to be a man he was very small and mean-looking. The mother always treated Luemba very well; but she maltreated Mavungu, and made him sleep outside the house beneath the mango trees. Often when he came to her, to beg for food, she would throw over his head the water in which she had cooked the beans.

Mavungu could not stand this bad treatment any longer; so he ran away into the woods, and wandered far away from home, until he came to a river. Here he found a canoe which he used to carry him still further from his town. And he paddled and paddled, until he came to a huge tree, that so overspread the river that he could not paddle any further. So he laid his paddle down, and caught hold of the leaves of the fuba tree to pull his canoe along. But no sooner had he begun to pull the leaves of the fuba tree, than he heard a voice, as if of a woman, faintly crying:

51

The Woman and Mavungu

"You are hurting me! please take care."

Mavungu wondered, but still pulled himself along.

"Take care! you are breaking my legs off," said the voice.

Still Mavungu pulled until a leaf broke off and suddenly changed into a beautiful woman. This startled Mavungu, so that he pulled many other leaves off the fuba tree. Each leaf turned into a man, or a woman; until his canoe was so full that he could not pull it.

Then the first woman told him that she had come to be his wife, and comfort him; and Mavungu was no longer afraid, but was very happy. Then the wife spoke to her fetish, and said:

"Am I to marry a man so ugly as this one is?"

And immediately Mavungu changed into a handsome man.

"Is he to be dressed like that?" she cried.

And straightway his dress was wonderfully changed.

In the same magical way the wife built Mavungu a large house and town for his people, so that he wanted nothing that was needful to a prince. And as people passed that way they were astonished at the change, and wondered where Mavungu had found his beautiful wife. And his mother and brother and whole family came to see him; and he treated them kindly and sent them away loaded with presents. But he had been told by his wife to say nothing to them as to the secret of his happiness. He, therefore, left them in ignorance of that fact.

Then his people invited Mavungu to their town, but his wife told him not to go, and so he stayed at home. But when he had received many invitations he finally agreed to visit them, in spite of his wife's advice. He promised, however, not to eat any of the food given to him. When he arrived in town his mother placed poisoned food before him and urged him to eat it, but he refused. They then asked about his beautiful wife, and, not thinking, he replied:

"Oh, when I left you I wandered through the woods."

But when he had got thus far he heard his wife's voice ringing through the woods:

"Oh! Ma-vu-ng-u-a-a-a!" and immediately he remembered, and got up and ran away home.

His wife was very cross with him, and told him plainly that she would not help him the next time he made a dunce of himself.

Some time after this Mavungu again went to visit his family. His wife said nothing, neither asking him to stay at home, nor giving him her consent to go. When he had greeted his mother and had eaten food, the family again asked him to tell them how he had found his wife.

And he said, "When I left you, because of your bad treatment, I wandered through the woods and came to a river. Dear me! where has my beautiful hat gone?"

"Your brother has taken it, to put it in the sun," said the mother, "but continue."

"I found a canoe with a paddle in it. Where has my coat gone?"

"Your brother has taken that also."

"And I paddled and paddled. Why have you taken my beautiful cloth?"

"To have it washed, of course."

"I paddled until I came to a big tree. Nay, why not leave me my shirt? And as I pulled off the leaves of the fuba tree, they turned into my wife and her companions. But I am naked!"

Then Mavungu remembered, and ran away to his town, only to find that it and his beautiful wife had disappeared. And when the people heard the whole story, they said it served Mavungu right for being so silly as to want to please his people, who had been his enemies all along, rather than please his wife, who had been so kind to him.

The Disobedient Daughter's Marriage

Effiong Edem lived in a small town. He had a very pretty daughter named Afiong. All the young men of the placed wanted to marry her on account of her beauty; but she refused all of them, although her parents told her not to be so haughty.

Afiong was very vain, and said she would only marry the best-looking man in the country. He would have to be young and strong and lovable. Most of the men whom her parents wanted her to marry were rich, but they were old and ugly. The girl, therefore, continued to disobey her parents. Her disobedience grieved them very much.

The Skull that lived in the spirit land heard of the beauty of this virgin, and decided that he would try to win her. To make a good appearance, then, he went among his friends and borrowed different parts of the body from them, all of the best. From one he got a good head, from another a body, from a third strong arms, and from a fourth a fine pair of legs. These parts made him a complete body and a fine-looking man. He next went from spirit land to the town market to see Afiong.

About this time Afiong heard that some one had seen in the market a very fine man who was better-looking than any of the men of that town. She therefore rushed to the market where she saw the Skull in his borrowed beauty. She fell in love with him at once and invited him to her home.

The Skull was delighted, and went home with her. When he arrived he was introduced by Afiong to her parents, and he immediately asked their consent to marry her. At first they refused, because they did not want her to marry a stranger; but at last they agreed.

The Skull lived with Afiong for two days in her parents' house. He then said he wished to take his wife back to his distant country. To this the girl readily agreed, because he was such a fine-looking man; but her parents tried to persuade her not to go. However, being very headstrong, she made up her mind to go, and they departed together.

After they had been gone a few days the father consulted the oracle and found out that his daughter's husband belonged to the spirit land, and that there she would surely die. They, therefore, all mourned her as dead.

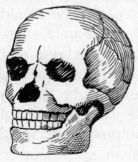

The Skull

After walking for several days, the bride and the groom crossed the border between the spirit land and the abode of human beings. Just as soon as they entered the spirit land, first of all one man came to the Skull and asked for his legs, then another for his head, and the next for his body, and so on, until in a few minutes the Skull was left by itself in all its natural ugliness.

At this the girl was very much frightened. She wanted to return home, but the Skull would not let her leave him, and ordered her to go with him.

When they arrived at the Skull's home they found his mother, who was a very old woman, too weak to do anything but to creep about. Afiong tried her best to help her. She cooked her food, and brought her water and firewood. The old creature was very grateful for these things, and soon began to like Afiong.

One day the old woman told Afiong that she was very very sorry for her, because all the people in the spirit land were cannibals. When they heard there was a human being in their country, they would come down and kill her and eat her. The old woman, then, hid Afiong.

Since Afiong had looked after her so well, the old woman promised that she would send her back to her home as soon as possible, if in the future she would obey her parents. This Afiong gladly agreed to do.

Then the old woman sent for the spider, which was a very clever hairdresser, and had him dress Afiong's hair in the latest style. She also gave

The Spider

her anklets and other things in return for her kindness. She then asked a spirit to call the winds to come and carry Afiong to her home.

At first a strong wind came, with thunder, lightning and rain; but the old woman sent it away because it was too rough. The next wind to come was a gentle breeze. She told the breeze to take Afiong to her mother's home, and said good-by to her. Very soon afterwards the breeze brought Afiong to the door of her parents' home, and left her there.

When the parents saw their daughter they were very glad, as they had long since given her up as dead. The father spread soft animals' skins on the ground from where his daughter was standing all the way to the house so that her feet should not be soiled. Afiong then walked to the house, and her father called all the young girls who belonged to Afiong's circle to come and dance, and the feasting and dancing continued for eight days and nights.

When the rejoicing was over, the father reported to the head chief of the town what had happened to Afiong. The chief then passed a law that parents should never allow their daughters to marry

A Dance

strangers who came from a distant land. Then the father told his daughter to marry a friend of his, and she willingly consented. Afiong lived with him for years, and they had many children.

Kindness Misunderstood

A woman went into the forest to seek fish in the streams. Seeing a stream with plenty of fish, she stopped, put her child down on the ground, took her flat basket, went down into the stream, and baled the water out of the stream. When it was dry she picked up the fish.

As she was stooping down to pick up the fish the child cried. An ape, hearing the cry of the child, came and held it in its arms and sang songs to it.

When the woman had finished picking up the fish she rose up to take the child and saw the animal carrying it. The mother wondered. She knew not what to do.

The ape spoke to the mother, saying, "Don't be afraid. I shall not harm you. I felt pity for your child because it was crying." And he said to the mother, "Take your child."

She took the child and went with it into the town, and said to her husband, "While I was picking up fish in the stream, an ape came and nursed the child and sang a song to it."

Her husband said to her, "That is not true."

But the wife replied, "Truly, it is not a falsehood. Want until tomorrow, and you will see."

In the morning the woman took the child and said to her husband, "Come along, let us go."

The husband took his spear. They walked along until they reached the stream. The wife put the child down and went into the stream, the husband hid himself in the bushes to see what would happen, and in a little while the child began to cry.

The ape, hearing the cry of the child, came and picked it up and sang a song to it. The child seemed to like the song and stopped crying.

When the husband saw this he threw his spear; the ape held out the child (to defend himself) and the spear went into the body of the child.

The ape said, "I felt pity for your child, and you have not killed me, but you have killed your child."

The Dog and the Leopard

It once happened that a leopard and a dog were very great friends; the leopard was, however, the owner of the house in which they lived; the dog was treated more as a servant than a friend by the leopard.

When the rainy season began, the leopard said to the dog, "Let us go and see our ant-hillocks, whether the ants are about to swarm, because the year is ended."

The dog agreed, and they went to look at the hillocks and found them showing signs of swarming. They, therefore, got ready and soon caught a large quantity of ants, which they took home. The leopard's wife cooked them, and they had a very fine meal. Those which they could not eat they fried and dried in the sun.

The leopard afterwards said, "I will take one bundle of these ants we have dried in the sun to my wife's relatives."

The dog agreed, and they set the day upon which they should go. Early in the morning of that day the leopard dressed in his best clothes and

The Leopard with the Dog carrying the Bundle of Ants

took his harp, because he was an expert player, and said to the dog, "You carry the ants."

The dog made the bundle into a load, put it on his head, and started off after the leopard. On the way they met some people they knew and greeted them.

Their friends asked them where they were going, and the leopard replied, "I am going to see my wife's relatives."

They asked him to play a tune on his harp, which he did, and sang, "I have a load of white ants like that which the dog carries; I have a load of white ants like that which the dog carries."

Their friends thanked the leopard for the tune and song, and took leave of him, and went on their way; and the leopard and the dog went on their way.

After a time the dog said, "Sir, I feel unwell; I must run aside into the grass."

The leopard said, "All right, go," and waited in the road for him.

While in the grass the dog ate all the ants and filled the packets with dry grass, and returned after tying them up as before. They then went on their way.

After a time the dog said to the leopard, "Sir, lend me the harp that I may play and sing as we walk."

The leopard did so, and the dog played and sang, "A load of rubbish for my wife's relations; a load of rubbish for my wife's relations."

The leopard thanked the dog for his song, and said, "You played very well."

To which the dog replied, "Thank you, sir."

When they reached the home of the relatives of the leopard's wife, the leopard greeted them and asked how they were. They also asked how the leopard and his wife and relatives were, but they took no notice of the dog. The leopard's relatives then brought out their pipes and gave the leopard one to smoke, but they did not give one to the dog.

After a time the dog walked away, and as soon as he got out of sight he ran away as fast as he could.

After a while the leopard said he had brought them some ants to eat, and began to untie the parcel, but to his surprise and disappointment he found nothing but dry grass. He was very angry and ashamed, and called for the dog; but the dog had gone.

When the leopard discovered how the dog had played him a trick and escaped, he went to the deity and consulted him about what he should do.

The deity answered, "When you beat the drums for twin dances the dog will come."

Some time later the leopard's wife gave birth to twins, and the leopard's friends and relatives came together and beat the drums for the twins, and danced; the sheep also came to the dance.

As they danced they sang, "Who will show me the dog? Who will show me the dog?"

Others took up the refrain and waved their tails,

saying, "There is no dog here, there is no dog here."

Late in the evening the sheep went home and told the dog about the dance, and what a wonderful entertainment it was.

The dog replied, "I am sorry I was not there to see it all."

The sheep said, "In the morning I will put you into my tail and take you."

The next morning the sheep put the dog into his tail, and they went to the dance. When the drums beat they all sang, "Show me the dog. Who will show me the dog?"

Others answered, "Here there is no dog, here there is no dog."

In the evening, when the drums were sounding loudly, the sheep became excited and danced and sang, and waved his tail so violently that the dog slipped out and fell to the ground. He immediately ran away, and again escaped. The leopard was very angry and caught the sheep and killed him. The dog ran off to man and lived with him.

Now, whenever a leopard meets a dog, he kills it if he can. From that time, too, there has been enmity between the leopard and the dog, and also between the sheep and the leopard because the sheep shielded the dog.

How the Dog Became the Friend of Man

The dog and the jackal were once brothers and lived together in the forest. One day they had had very poor luck at hunting; and, as night fell, they were hungry and shivering with cold.

"Jackal!" called the dog.

"What do you want?" said the jackal.

"A man has a home nearby," said the dog.

"I know," said the jackal.

"A fire is burning in his house," said the dog.

"Yes."

"Fire is nice and warm."

"Yes."

"There may be a bone lying near the fire."

"Yes."

"Why don't you go and get some fire and the bone?" "Not I," said the jackal. "If you want these things go and get them yourself."

"I am afraid," said the dog and laid himself down to sleep.

As it was getting colder and colder, however, the dog's teeth began to chatter, because the dog had less fur than the jackal and felt the cold more keenly. At last he could bear it no longer and said, "I will go and get fire; you stay, and, if I don't come back soon, you come and call me."

"Yes," said the jackal.

Off went the dog to the village, but as he was getting near it he disturbed the man's fowls with a noise. The man came out with his spear, then, to kill the intruder.

The dog pleaded for mercy. "Please don't kill me!" said he; "I am a poor beast dying of cold and starvation; let me warm myself by your fire and then I will return to the forest."

The Dog and the Jackal

"Let it be so," said the man. "Warm yourself, but when you have done so, back you must go to the forest!"

The dog entered the hut and lay down near the warm fire. He picked up a bone the man had thrown away and began to gnaw it. After a time the man asked,

"Have you finished?"

The Dog gnawing a bone by the fire in the Man's hut

"Not yet," said the dog as he started on another bone. After a time the man asked again, "Have you finished?"

"Not yet," replied the dog, looking for another bone.

The fire was warm and the bone tasted good. The dog felt happier than he had ever been before.

So when the man asked for the third time, "Have you finished?" the dog answered:

"Yes, but I want you to keep me with you. I will be helpful: instead of killing your fowls like brother jackal, I will help you to catch the fowls of the jungle; I will show you all the cunning ways of the wild beasts. For my service I only ask you for a place near your hearth and the bones from your meal."

"Thus let it be," said the man; and since then the dog has lived with man.

As the night falls now you will hear a plaintive howl in the bush, "Bo-a, bo-a" (dog, dog!). That is the jackal calling for his brother.

The Cats and Fowls

At one time the fowls used to be lords of the wild cats, and made them their servants, who had to supply them with food. Whenever a cat caught flying ants, the fowls took almost all they caught. The ants were put in large packets, which the cats had to tie up and bring before the fowls to let them see what they had taken.

The Cat finds the Fowl asleep

The cats did not like this task, and once or twice they wanted to stop doing it, but were afraid because the fowls threatened to burn them with their combs. The cats believed that the comb of the fowl was flaming fire. But one day the cats' fire had gone out, and a mother cat sent one of the younger members of the family to the fowls to beg for fire.

When the young cat arrived, he found the rooster very drunk and fast asleep, and the others away from home. He tried to wake him, but failed to do so. He, therefore, went back and told his mother.

The mother said, "Go back again with some dry grass and put it to his comb and bring the fire."

So he went back and applied the grass to the comb, but there was no fire.

The young cat came back to his mother and told her the grass would not take fire; the mother was angry and said, "You have not really tried; come along with me and do it again."

When they went again, the rooster was still asleep. They crept up to him very slowly, and touched the comb with the grass, and then blew on it to see if it was on fire, but there was never a spark. They felt it to see whether or not the comb was hot, putting their hands gently on it, thought they were very much afraid of being burnt.

To their great surprise they found that the comb was very cold, even though it was red. After feeling it they finally waked the fowl and told him they were not going to serve him any longer. They were tired of his rule.

The fowl was angry and began to make a great noise, and tried to frighten the cats with threats, but they said, "We don't fear you; we have tested your comb while you were asleep and know that it has no fire in it, and now we will kill you if you say anything more."

The fowl saw that his empty boasting had been exposed, and from that time fowls have had to escape cats because of the enmity between them.

Boasting is not courage.

He who boasts much cannot do much.

Boasting at home is not valor; parade is not battle; when war comes the brave will be known.

Be courageous if you would be true. Truth and courage go together.

Lies, however numerous, will be caught by truth when it rises up. The voice of truth is easily known.

The laborer is always in the sun; the landowner is always in the shade.

To love the king is not bad, but a king who loves you is better.

Why Chickens Live with Man

All the birds lived in a certain part of the kingdom of Njambi, the Master of all. The pelicans, chickens, eagles, parrots and all other winged kinds all lived together, separated from other animals.

One day, some one asked the question, "Who is the king of the birds?" Each one named himself the king of the birds. The chicken said, "I!" the parrot, "I!" the eagle, "I!" and so on. Every day they had this same dispute. They were not able to settle it, or to agree to choose any one of their number as king.

They said, then, "Let us go to Njambi, and ask him."

They agreed; and all went to him so that he might say who was the greatest among them.

When they all had arrived at Njambi's town, he asked, "What is the affair on which you have come?"

They answered, "We have come, not for a visit, but for a purpose. We have a dispute among ourselves. We wish to know, of all the birds, who is the chief. Each one says for himself that he is the greatest of all. This one, because he knows how to fly well; that one because he can speak well; and another one, because he is strong. But, of these

74

three things, flight, speech, and strength, we ask you, which is the greatest?"

At once all the birds cried out to Njambi, each one saying, "Choose me; I know how to speak!"

The Speaking Contest among the Birds

Njambi quieted them, and said, "Well, then, come here! I know that you all speak. But, show me, each one of you, your manner of speaking."

The eagle, then, stood up to be examined.

Njambi asked him, "How do you speak? What is your manner of talking?"

The eagle began to scream, "So-o-we! so-o-we! so-o-we!"

Njambi said, "Good! Now call me your wife!"

The wife of the eagle came, and Njambi said to her, "You are the wife of the eagle; how do you talk?"

The wife replied, "I say, 'So-o-we! so-o-we! so-o-we!'"

Njambi said to the eagle, "Indeed! you and your wife speak the same kind of language."

The eagle answered, "Yes; my wife and I speak alike."

They were told to stand aside.

Then Njambi said, "Bring me here the parrot." And he asked, "Parrot, how do you talk? What is your way of speaking?"

The parrot squawked, "I say, 'Ko-do-ko!'"

Njambi then said, "Well, call me your wife!"

She came; and he asked her, "How do you talk? Talk now!"

The wife said, "I say, 'Ko-do-ko!'"

Njambi asked the parrot, "So! your wife says, 'Ko-do-ko!'"

The parrot answered, "Yes; my wife and I both say, 'Ko-do-ko!'"

Njambi then said, "Call me here the plantain-eater."

He came, and was asked, "And how do you talk?"

He shouted, "I say, 'Mbru-kâ-kâ! mbru-kâ-kâ! mbru!'"

Njambi told him to call his wife. She came, and, when asked, spoke in the same way as her husband. Njambi sent them away, saying, "Good! you and your wife say the same thing. Good!"

All the birds, then, in succession, were summoned; and they all, husband and wife, had the same manner of speaking, except one who had not been called.

Njambi finally said, "Call the chicken here!"

The rooster stood up, and strutted forward.

Njambi asked him, "What is your speech? Show me your mode of talking!"

The rooster threw up his head, stretched his throat, and crowed, "Kâ-kâ-re-kââ."

Njambi said, "Good! Bring your wife hither."

The hen came; and, of her, Njambi asked, "And, what do you say?"

She replied, "My husband told me that I might talk only if I bore children. So when I lay an egg, I say, 'Kwa-ka! kwa-ka!'"

Njambi exclaimed, "So! you don't say, 'Kâ-kâ-re-kââ,' as your husband does?"

She replied, "No, I do not talk as he does."

Then Njambi said to the rooster, "Why do you not allow your wife to say, 'Kâ-kâ-re-kââ?'"

The rooster replied, "I am a chicken, I respect myself. I jeer at all these other birds. They and their wives speak in the same way. A visitor, if he comes to their towns, is not able to know, when one of them speaks, which is husband and which is wife, because they both speak alike. But the wife of a rooster is unable to speak as he does. I do not allow it. A husband should be at the head; and in his wife it is not becoming for her to be equal with him or to talk as well as he does."

Njambi listened to this long speech; and then asked, "Have you finished?"

The chicken answered, "Yes."

Njambi summoned all the birds to stand together in one place near him, and he said, "The affair which you brought to me, I settle it thus: The chicken is your head, because you others all speak, husband and wife, each alike. But, he speaks for himself in his own way, and his wife in her way to show that a husband is the head of his home. Therefore, as he knows how to be head of his family, it is settled that the chicken is the head also of your tribe."

But Njambi went on to say, "Though this is true, you, chicken, don't you go back again into the forest, to your kingship of the birds. For the other birds will be jealous of you. You are not strong, you cannot fight them all. Lest they kill you, stay with me in my town."

Why the Hawk Catches Chickens

In the olden days there was a very fine young hen that lived with her parents in the forest. One day a hawk was flying around, about eleven o'clock in the morning, as was his custom. He made large circles in the air almost without moving his wings. His keen eyes were wide open. They took in everything, for nothing moving ever escapes the eyes of a hawk, no matter how small it may be or how high up in the air the hawk may fly.

This hawk saw the pretty hen picking up grains of corn near her father's home. He thereupon closed his wings slightly, and in a second of time was near the ground. He then spread his wings out to check his flight. He alighted close to the hen on a high rock, as a hawk does not like to walk on the ground if he can hop along on something else.

He then greeted the young hen in his most charming manner and offered to marry her. She agreed. The hawk, then, spoke to the parents, and paid mostly in corn the dowry which they asked. The next day the hawk took the young hen off to his home.

Soon thereafter a young rooster that lived near the hen's former home found out where she was

The Hawk on a high rock

living. He had been in love with her for some months, ever since his spurs had grown. He thought he would try to make her return to her own home. He, therefore, went at dawn to the hawk's home, flapped his wings once or twice, and crowed in his best voice to the young hen. When she heard the sweet voice of the rooster she could not resist his invitation. She went out to him, and they walked off together to her parents' house. The young rooster went strutting in front, stopping to crow from place to place.

The hawk, although flying high up in the sky, far out of sight of the human eye, saw what had happened, and was very angry. He made up his mind at once that he would obtain justice from the king. He flew off to the king of birds and told him the whole story, and asked for justice.

The king sent for the parents of the hen, and told them that, according to native custom, they must pay back the dowry they had received from the hawk when he married their daughter; but the hen's parents said that they were so poor that they were not able to pay it.

The king, then, told the hawk that whenever and wherever he found any of the rooster's children he could kill and eat any of them as payment of his

The Rooster and Hen

dowry; and, if the rooster made any complaint, the king would not listen to it.

From that time until now, whenever a hawk sees a chicken he swoops down and carries it off in part-payment of his dowry which should have been returned long ago.

African Words of Wisdom

He who marries a beauty marries trouble.

Quick loving a woman means quick not loving a woman. ("Marry in haste and repent at leisure.")

When a person hates you, he will beat your animals.

The hawk having caught my chicken will not stay because it knows it has done (wrong).

When the hawk hovers over the yard the owner of the fowls feel uneasy.

No one would expose fowls on the top of a rock in the sight of a hawk.

Hawks go away for the nesting season and fools think they have gone forever.

A bird walking nevertheless has wings.

The Fox and the Goat

The fox and the goat went to a big meeting, and they were put together in one house. The fox and the goat got into a quarrel. The goat, then, told the fox that he intended to get him into a trouble out of which he would never be able to escape.

The Goat meets the Leopard.

The fox said, "All right; you put trouble on me, and I will return the same to you."

The goat went for a walk, and he saw a leopard, and being frightened, he asked, "Auntie, what are you doing here?"

"My little one is sick," said the old leopard.

The goat then said, "The fox has medicine that will make your little one well."

83

The leopard said, "All right, you go and call him."

So the goat went to the fox and said, "They call you."

"Who calls me?" replied the fox.

"I do not know," said the goat; "I think it is your friend. You take this path and you will meet him."

The fox went down the path, and at length came upon the leopard. The fox became frightened and inquired, "Did you call me?"

"Yes, my son; your brother is sick. The goat came just a while ago and told me you had medicine that would make my little one well."

The Fox meets the Leopard.

"Yes," said the fox, "I have medicine that will cure your little one, but I must have a little goat horn to put in it. If you get me a goat horn I will let you have the medicine."

"Which way did the goat go?" asked the leopard.

"I left him up there," replied the fox.

"You wait here with my little one, and I will bring you the horn," said the leopard.

"All right," said the fox, and away went the leopard.

In a little while the leopard killed the goat and returned with his horns to the fox. You are liable to fall in the trap you set for someone else.

Wit of Africans

1. Ordinary people are as common as grass,
   But good people are dearer than the eye.

2. A matter dealt with gently is sure to prosper,
   But a matter dealt with violently causes vexation.

3. Familiarity breeds contempt,
   But distance secures respect.

4. Anger does nobody good,
   But patience is the father of kindness.
   Anger draws arrows from the quiver,
   But good words draw kola-nuts from the bag.

5. A fruitful woman is the enemy of the barren,
   And an industrious man is the foe of the lazy.

6. Beg for help, and you will meet with refusals;
   Ask for alms and you will meet with misers.

7. Today is the elder brother of tomorrow,
   And a heavy dew is the elder brother of rain.

8.   Birth does not differ from birth;
     As the free man was born so was the slave.

9.   My badness is more manifest than my
     goodness;
     You look up my goodness in the room,
     And you sell my badness in the market.

10. Know thyself better than he who speaks of
     thee.
     Not to know is bad, not to wish to know is
     worse.

Why Goats Live with Man

The goat and his mother lived alone in their village. He said to her, "I have here a magic-medicine to make one strong in wrestling. There is no one who can overcome me, or cast me down; I can overcome any other person."

The other beasts heard of this boast; and they took up the challenge. First, house-rats, hundreds of them, came to the goat's village, to wrestle with him. He overcame two hundred of them one by one. The rats, then, went back to their places, saying that they were not able to overcome the goat.

Then the forest-rats came to wrestle with the goat. He overcame them also in the same way. And they went back to their own place defeated.

Then the antelopes came to wrestle with the goat. He overcame all the antelopes, every one of them; not one was able to throw the goat to the ground. And they also went back to their places disappointed.

Also, the elephant with all the elephants came on that same mission. The goat overcame all the elephants; and they, too, went back to their place defeated.

Thus, all the beasts came, in the same way, and were also overcome by the goat, and went back surprised at the goat's strength.

The Goat and the Mother

But there still remained one beast, only one, the leopard. He had not made the attempt. He said he would go, as he was sure he could overcome. He came, but the goat overcame him also. It was proved, then, that not a single beast could withstand the goat. This made the goat think that he was king.

Then the father of all the leopards said: "I am ashamed that this beast should overcome me. I will kill him!"

And he thought of a plan to do so. He went to the spring where mankind got their drinking water and stood, hiding at the spring. When men of the town went to the spring to get water the leopard killed two of them.

The people went to tell the goat, "Go away from here, for the leopard is killing mankind on your account."

The mother of the goat said to him, "If that is so, let us go to my brother, the antelope." So they both went to the uncle antelope.

When they came to his village, they told him their errand.

He bravely said, "Remain here! Let me see the leopard come here with his boldness!"

They were then at the antelope's village about two days. On the third day, about eight o'clock in the morning, the leopard came there as if for a walk. When the antelope saw him, the goat and his mother hid themselves; and the antelope asked the leopard, "What is your anger? Why are you angry with my nephew?"

At that very moment, while the antelope was speaking, the leopard seized him on the ear. The antelope cried out, "What are you killing me for?"

The leopard replied, "Show me the place where the goat and his mother are."

So the antelope, being afraid, said, "Come to-night, and I will show you where they sleep. And you may kill them; but don't kill me."

While he was saying this, the goat overheard, and said to his mother, "We must flee, lest the leopard kill us."

At sundown, then, that evening, the goat and his mother fled to the village of the elephant.

About midnight, the leopard came to the antelope's village, as he had been told, and looked for the goat, but did not find him. The leopard went to all the houses of the village, and when he came to the antelope's home, in his disappointment he killed him.

The leopard kept up his search, and set out to find where the goat had gone. Following the footprints, he came to the village of the elephant.

When he arrived there, the elephant demanded, "What's the matter?"

And the same conversation followed, as at the antelope's village, and with the same result. The elephant was killed by the leopard, for the goat and his mother had fled, and had gone to the village of the ox.

The leopard followed, and came to the village of the ox. There all the same things happened, as in the other villages. The goat and his mother fled, and the ox was killed by the leopard.

Then the mother, wearying of flight and sorry that she had caused their friends to be killed, said, "My child! if we continue to flee to the villages of other beasts the leopard will follow, and will kill them. Let us flee to the homes of mankind."

They fled again, then, and came to the town of man, and told him their story. He received them kindly. He took the goat and his mother as guests, and gave them a house to live in.

Not long afterward the leopard came to the town of man looking for the goat.

But the man said to the leopard, "Those beasts whom you killed failed to find a way in which to kill you. But, if you come here, we will find a way."

So that night, then, the leopard went back to the village. The man then made a big trap for the

He saw an open way to a small house.

leopard, with two rooms in it. He took the goat and put him in one room of the trap.

Night came. The leopard left his village, still going to seek the goat; and he came again to the town of man. The leopard stood still, listened, and sniffed the air. He smelled the odor of the goat, and was glad, and said, "So! this night I will get him!"

He saw an open way to a small house. He thought it was a door. He entered, and was caught in the trap. He could see the goat through the cracks of the wall, but could not get at him.

The goat jeered at him, "My friend! you were about to kill me, but you are unable."

Daybreak came. And people of man's town found the leopard in the trap, caught fast. They took machetes and guns, and killed him.

Then man said to the goat, "You shall not go back to the forest; remain here always. Some friend or relative of the leopard may try to kill you."

This is the reason that goats like to live with mankind, through fear of leopards.

Hints to the Wise

The sun is the king of torches.

Ashes fly back in the face of him that throws them.

When the cat dies the mice rejoice.

A man falls into the trap he sets for others.

Faults are like a hill; you stand on your own and you talk about those of other people.

Do not repair another man's fence until you have seen to your own.

The Lion, the Leopard, and the Dog

The lion, the leopard, and the dog were living together. They heard the news that the goat had built a big town.

The lion said to the leopard, "We had better wage war on that town, as we have nothing to eat."

So the two joined and carried on war against goat-town. They fought a whole day but were unable to take the town and were driven back.

They went back and told the dog of their misfortune and that he must join them in another attempt to take goat-town. The next morning the three went, and after fighting all day they took the town.

When they went into the town they found only one goat and one cat. The lion caught the goat and the cat and said they were going to carry them away. The cat did not wish to be tied, and asked to be left untied so that he could dance.

The lion said, "All right."

Then the goat said, "You should leave me untied as I am a doctor."

So they left both untied.

"Let me see you dance now," said the lion. The cat began to dance and he danced well.

93

Then he said, "I can jump."

"Jump then," said the lion. The cat jumped over the barricade and ran into the bush.

The lion turned to the goat and said, "You say you are a doctor. Well, the cat has run away. I want you to try your medicine, so that we can catch him."

Then the lion, the leopard, and the dog all closed up around the goat to prevent his getting away as the cat had done.

*Then the Lion, the Leopard, and the Dog all closed
up around the Goat.*

The goat told the lion to bring him one large pot. The pot was brought. The goat put his hand in his bag, and he took out one bottle filled with honey. He placed the honey in the pot.

"You must put a cloth over me and the pot," said the goat.

The lion did not know that the goat had honey; he thought it was water in the pot.

The goat took a spoon and gave the lion some of the honey in the pot, saying, "This is some of the water my medicine gave me."

When the lion tasted the honey he said, "Oh, you are a doctor for true."

The lion said, "I know you are a doctor now, so make me some medicine to wear around my neck."

The goat told the lion that the medicine they wear around the neck is put up in leopard skin, and that he must kill the leopard so he could get some of the skin.

"All right," said the lion.

The lion started after the leopard, and the leopard ran, and the lion after him, and the dog followed. So the goat made his escape back the other way.

So the lion dislikes the leopard, the leopard dislikes the goat, and the goat dislikes the dog.

More Words of Wisdom

1. There is no medicine for hate.
2. He is a heathen who bears malice.
3. Wrangling is the father of fighting.
4. Men despise what they do not understand.
5. He who injures another brings injury upon himself.
6. Hate the evil which a man does but do not hate the man himself.
7. The evil doer is ever anxious.
8. If you love yourself others will hate you;
   If you humble yourself others will love you.

The Leopard, the Tortoise, and the Bush Rat

Once there was a great famine on earth, and all the animals were very thin and weak from want of food; but there was one exception, and that was the tortoise and all his family. They were very fat, and did not seem to suffer at all. Even the leopard was very thin, in spite of the promise of animals to bring him other animals for food.

In the early days of the famine the leopard had killed the mother of the tortoise. The tortoise, then, was very angry with the leopard, and intended if possible to be even with him. The tortoise was very clever and had discovered a shallow lake full of fish in the middle of the forest. Every morning he used to go to the lake and bring back enough fish for himself and his family. One day the leopard met the tortoise and noticed how fat he was. As he

The Tortoise on the way

was very thin himself he decided to watch the tortoise. The next morning, then, the leopard hid himself in the long grass near the

96

home of the tortoise and waited, until the tortoise came along with a heavy basket. Then the leopard jumped out, and said to the tortoise:

"What have you in that basket?"

The tortoise did not want to lose his breakfast, and would not tell what he was carrying; but the leopard could easily tell things by smell. He knew at once that there was fish in the basket. He then said:

"I know there is fish in there, and I am going to eat it."

The tortoise was afraid to refuse. As he was such a poor creature, he said:

"Very well. Let us sit down under this shady tree, and if you will make a fire I will go to my home and get pepper, oil, and salt, and then

The Leopard began to search about for dry wood.

we will eat together. Isn't that fair enough for both of us?"

The leopard agreed to do this and began to search about for dry wood to start the fire. While the leopard was doing this the tortoise moved slowly off to his house, and very soon came back with the pepper, salt, and oil. He also brought a long piece of cane tie-tie, which is very strong. He put this on the ground, and began boiling the fish. Then he said to the leopard:

"While we are waiting for the fish to cook, let us play at tying one another up to a tree. You may tie me up first, and when I say, 'Tighten,' you must loose the rope, and when I say 'Loosen,' you must tighten the rope."

The leopard was very hungry, but he thought that this game would make the time pass more quickly while the fish was being cooked. He, therefore, agreed to play.

The tortoise then stood with his back to the tree and said: "Loosen the rope." The leopard, as he had agreed, began to tie up the tortoise.

Very soon the tortoise cried out: "Tighten!" The leopard at once unfastened the tie-tie, and the tortoise was free.

The tortoise then said,

"Now, leopard, it is your turn."

The leopard, then, stood up against the tree and called out to the tortoise to loosen the rope, and the tortoise at once very quickly passed the rope several times around the leopard and got him fast to the tree. Then the leopard said, "Tighten the rope."

But instead of playing the game as he said he would, the tortoise ran faster and faster with the rope round the leopard. He took care to keep out of reach of the leopard's claws, and very soon had the leopard fastened so tight that he could not get away.

All this time the leopard was crying out to the tortoise to let him go, as he was tired of the game; but the tortoise only laughed, and sat down at the fireside and commenced his meal. When he had finished eating all he wanted, he picked up the remainder of the fish for his family, and made ready to go. Before he started, however, he said to the leopard:

"You killed my mother and now you want to take my fish. It is not likely that I am going to the lake to get fish for you, so I shall leave you here to starve."

All that day and throughout the night the leopard was yelling for some one to let him loose; but no one came, because the people and animals of the forest do not like to hear the leopard's voice.

In the morning, when the animals began to go out to find food, the leopard begged every one he saw to come and untie him; but they all refused, as they knew that if they did so the leopard would most likely kill them at once and eat them.

At last a bush rat came by and saw the leopard tied up to the tree and asked him what his trouble was. The leopard told him that he had been playing a game of "tight" and "loose" with the tortoise, and that he had tied him up and left him there to starve. The leopard then begged the bush rat to cut the ropes with his sharp teeth.

The bush rat was very sorry for the leopard; but at the same time he knew that, if he let the leopard go, the leopard would most likely kill and eat the one that had thus done him a kind act. He therefore hesitated, and said that he did not quite see his way clear to cut the ropes.

But this bush rat was very kind-hearted. He had had some experience with traps himself, and could sympathize with the leopard in his pain. The bush rat therefore thought for a time, and then made a plan. He first started to dig a hole under the tree. When he had finished the hole he came out and cut one of the ropes, and immediately ran into his hole, and waited there to see what would happen; but although the leopard struggled very much, he could not get loose, as the tortoise had tied him up so fast. After a time, when he saw that there was no danger, the bush rat crept out again and very carefully bit through another rope, and then came back to his hole as before. Again nothing happened, and he began to feel safe. He then bit several strands through one after the other until the last rope was cut and the leopard was free.

The Bush Rat

The leopard was wild with hunger. Instead of being grateful to the bush rat, as soon as the leopard was free he made a dash at the bush rat with his big paw, but just missed him, as the bush rat had dived for his hole. The bush rat, however, was not quick enough to escape the leopard's paw, and the sharp claws scratched his back and left marks which all bush rats carry even to this day.

The Lioness and the Cow

There were once a lioness and a cow living near to each other, though not in the same house; the lioness gave birth to a baby lioness, and the cow gave birth to a male calf. When the two children grew up the cow's child was mischievous, while the lioness's child was gentle and meek.

After a time the cow and the lioness dug a well, and got it into splendid order.

The lioness said to the cow, "We have an excellent well, but you can't imagine how full of mischief your son is; so please warn him lest he come and spoil our well, and cause us to quarrel and end our friendship." The cow agreed to do so.

Soon after this the lioness went away to obtain food, and asked the cow to look after her child while she was away. The cow consented to do so, and the two children played together near the house for some time. Presently they went farther away and came to the well. The calf first knocked some dirt into it, and after further play he pushed the baby lioness into the well and she was drowned.

The calf ran home to his mother and said his companion had fallen into the well and was drowned.

The cow said, "The lioness will surely kill me for this; let us run away."

They packed up hastily, then ran away to the bush buck, and hid with him. The bush buck made them welcome and promised to butt the lioness and drive her away should she come.

When the lioness came back from seeking food she found the house empty, and went on to the cow's house, but that was also empty. She then hunted about and called, but got no reply. After a

The Lioness and the Dead Cub

long search she came upon the body of her child in the well, and wept bitterly and bemoaned her loss. She then hunted the cow and at length came to the bush buck, calling:

"Whose, whose?"

To this the bush buck answered, "Yours, yours."

The bush buck said to the cow, "Run away, you will cause me my death; run away to the antelope."

The cow did so, and hid there for a time; but when the antelope said:

"Run away, you are bringing me into trouble and will cause my death."

The cow fled to the elephant and hid with him, but when the lioness came and found her and roared, the elephant said:

Running from the Lioness

"Run away from here, you are bringing me into trouble and will be the cause of my death."

Again, then, she had to flee.

It thus came about that the cow had constantly to run away from the lioness, and was always in fear. One day as she was fleeing away she met a Wakasanke bird which asked her why she was always running away in this manner.

The cow answered:

"Because my child killed the child of the lioness and she wants to kill me, and I am looking for a place where I may be safe from her wrath."

The Wakasanke replied:

"Stay with me, I will frighten the lioness and drive her away."

The Lioness running away

The cow gladly agreed, and stayed.

Wakasanke made ready to receive the lioness. He first brought a flower of the plantain, which is shaped like the heart of an animal and of a reddish-brown color. This he put ready. He then milked some milk into a pot and put that near; he next drew a pot of blood from the cow and put that also ready. When all his preparations were made he waited.

After a time the lioness came and cried, "Whose, whose?"

Wakasanke answered, "Mine, mine," and took the pot of blood and dashed it on the lioness's breast and said, "I have killed you, is not this your blood?" He struck the lioness with the flower, shouting, "Is not that your heart? I have killed you. I have killed you." He then took the pot of milk and dashed it with all his force upon the lioness's head, saying, "Let me crush in your head and brains and finish you off."

In this way he so terrified the lioness that she thought it was her blood, and she rushed away leaving the cow in peace.

Thus Wakasanke birds have lived about cows, and every herdsman when he goes to milk his cow, first milks a little on the ground to commemorate the action of the Wakasanke bird. From that time whenever a lion meets a cow the lion tries to kill it.

Why the Hippopotamus
Lives in the Water

A long time ago the hippopotamus, whose name was Isantim, was one of the biggest kings on the land. He was second only to the elephant. The hippo had seven large, fat female servants, of whom he was very fond. One of them he called his wife.

Now and then he used to give a big feast to the people; but a curious thing was that, although every one knew the hippo, no one, except his wife and servants, knew his name.

At one of the feasts, just as the people were about to sit down, the hippo said:

"You have come to feed at my table, but none of you know my name. If you cannot tell my name, you shall all of you go away without your dinner."

As they could not guess his name, they had to go away and leave all the good food behind them. But before they left, the tortoise arose and asked the hippopotamus what he would do if some one told him his name at the next feast?

The hippo said that he would be so ashamed of himself that he and his whole family would leave the land and for the future would dwell in the water.

Now it was the custom for the hippo and his wife and servants to go down every morning and evening to the river to wash and drink. The tortoise knew this was their custom. The hippo used to walk first, and the wife and servants followed.

One day when they had gone down to the river to bathe, the tortoise made a small hole in the middle of the path, and there waited. When the hippo and his companions returned, one of them and his wife were some distance behind. The tortoise came out from where he had been hiding, and half

The party at the stream

buried himself in the hole he had dug, leaving the larger part of his shell outside.

When the two companions came along, the wife knocked her foot against the tortoise's shell, and immediately called out to her husband, "Oh! Isantim, my husband, I have hurt my foot."

At this the tortoise was very glad, and went joyfully home, as he had found out the hippo's name.

When the next feast was given by the hippo, he made the same condition about his name; so the tortoise got up and said, "You promise you will not harm me if I tell you your name?" and the hippo promised.

The tortoise then shouted as loud as he was able, "Your name is Isantim," at which a cheer went up from all the people, and then they sat down to their dinner.

When the feast was over, the hippo, with his wife and servants, in accordance with his promise went down to the river, and they have always lived in the water from that day till now; and although they come on shore to feed at night, you never find a hippo on the land in the daytime.

For Children

There is no wealth without children.

It is the duty of children to wait on elders, not elders on children.

If you love the children of others you will love your own even better.

Distress carries off him whose mother is no more.

Bowing to a dwarf will not prevent your standing erect again.

"I have forgotten your name" is better than "I know thee not."

Why the Bush Fowl Calls up the Dawn

A man once went into the bush with his wife to collect palm nuts. He saw a palm with ripe clusters upon it, and climbed it to get them. While he was trying to cut through the stems, a black fly began to buzz round him, dash into his eyes, against his nose, and all over his face. He lifted his hand to drive it away, and as he did so he dropped the knife.

"Run, run," he called to his wife, who was just beneath the tree, for he feared that it might fall upon her. She sprang aside so quickly that she was out of the way before the knife reached the ground.

In her haste she jumped over a serpent. This startled it so that it dived down a brown rat's hole, and begged for a drink of water. The rat handed the serpent a calabash full, and the serpent drank it all at once. The rat was so frightened at such a thing that it sprang past the serpent out of the hole and ran up a tree, where it sat trembling. The place where the rat had stopped was near a plantain-eater's nest. No sooner did the latter see the rat than it raised a cry. This startled a monkey, which rushed forth ready for a fight.

In his haste to meet his enemy, the monkey sprang on to a ripe fruit of the tree called Ntun. This fell from its stalk onto the back of an elephant which was passing beneath. The animal rushed away in such terror, that it tore down and carried off a flowering creeper which caught round his neck.

The creeper in turn pulled over an ant hill, which fell on the bush fowl's nest, and broke its eggs.

The bush fowl was so sad because of the loss, that it sat brooding over the crushed eggs, and forgot to call the dawn. For two days, therefore, the whole world was in darkness.

All the beasts wondered what could be the reason of this continued night, and at length Obassi called them before him to find out the cause.

When all were present Obassi asked the bush fowl why it was now forty-eight hours since it had called for light. Then the bush fowl stood forth and answered:

"My eggs were broken by the ant hill, which was pulled over by the creeper, which was dragged down by the elephant, which was knocked over by the Ntun fruit, which was plucked by the monkey, which was frightened by the plantain-eater, which was startled by the rat, which was scared by the serpent, which had been jumped over by a sick woman, who had been made to run by the fall of a knife, which had been dropped by her husband, who had been bitten by a black fly. Angry,

therefore, on account of the loss of the eggs, I refused to call the day."

Each was asked in turn to give the reason for
the damage it had done, and each in turn gave the
same long answer, till it came to the turn of the
black fly, the first cause of all the mischief. Instead
of answering properly, as the others had done, the
black fly only said, "Buzz, buzz." So Obassi commanded the fly to remain speechless forevermore,
and to do nothing but buzz about and be present
wherever a rotten thing lies.

To the bush fowl he said that at once it should
call the long-delayed dawn, and never again refuse
to do so, whether its eggs were broken or not. Day
must dawn.

Why the Cat Catches Rats

Ansa was king of Calabar for fifty years. He had a very faithful cat as a housekeeper and a rat as his house-boy. The king was an obstinate, headstrong man; but he was very fond of the cat, for she had been in his store for many years.

The rat fell in love with one of the king's servant girls; but he was poor and could not give her any presents. What, then, would he do?

At last he thought of the king's store. In the night-time, as he was quite small, he had little difficulty in getting into the store through a hole he had made in the roof. He then stole corn and native pears, and gave them to the girl he loved.

At the end of the month, when the cat had to give the king her account of the things in the store, it was found that some corn and native pears were not there. The king was very angry at this, and asked the cat how this happened. But the cat could not explain the loss, until one of

The Cat and the Rat

114

her friends told her
that the rat had been
taking the corn and
giving it to the girl.

When the cat told
the king, he called the
girl before him and
had her whipped. He
turned the rat over
to the cat to be pun-
ished and he then

The Cat catches the Rat.

drove both of them from his home. The cat was so
angry at this that she killed and ate the rat. Ever
since then whenever a cat sees a rat she tries to
kill and eat it.

Thoughts About Animals

1. When the rat laughs at the cat, there is a hole.
    The rat has not power to call the cat to
    account.
    The rat does not go to sleep in the cat's bed.
2. If the dog is not at home he barks not.
    A heedless dog will not do for the chase.
    A lurking dog does not lie in the hyena's lair.
3. He who cannot move an ant, and yet tries to
    move an elephant, shall find out his folly.
    The elephant does not find his trunk heavy.
    If there were no elephant in the jungle the buf-
    falo would be a great animal.

4. The butterfly that brushes against thorns will tear its wings.
5. If the fly flies, the frog goes not supperless to bed.
6. When the fox dies fowls do not mourn.
7. When the goat goes abroad, the sheep must run.
8. He who goes with a wolf will learn to howl.

The Crocodile's Relatives

A long time ago the crocodile became very old and died. News of his death was carried from one to another until all the beasts of the forests knew it.

After his funeral, the animals thought of dividing his property. At once a quarrel arose. The property belonged to the crocodile's nearest relatives, but too many animals said they were his kin and asked for their part of the property.

The birds said, "He was our kin and we shall divide the property."

Others said, no, and asked, "On what ground do you claim to be kin to the crocodile? You wear feathers; you do not wear plates of armor as he does."

The birds replied, "True enough, he did not wear our feathers; but, you are not to judge by what he had on in his life. Judge by what he was in the beginning of his life. Look you! In his beginning, he began life as an egg. We believe in eggs. His mother bore him as an egg. He is our relative, and we should have his property."

But the beasts said, "It shall not be so! We are his relatives. We shall have his property divided."

The Crocodile

To settle the quarrel it was necessary for the animals to hold a council. The council of animals then asked the beasts why they said that they were relatives of the crocodile, and what they had to say about the crocodile's egg origin.

The beasts responded:

"It may be true that the mark of tribe must be found, in a beginning; but it is not in an egg, for all beings began as eggs. Life is the original beginning. Look you! When life really begins in the egg, then the mark of tribe is shown. When the crocodile's life began, he had four legs as we have. We judge by legs. So we claim him as our relative. And we shall take his property."

But the birds answered:

"You beasts said we were not his relatives, because we wear feathers, and not crocodile plates. But, you, look you! Judge by our own words. Neither do you wear crocodile plates, you with your hair and fur! Your words are not correct. The beginning of his life was not, as you say, when the little crocodile sprouted some legs. There was life in the egg before that. And his egg was like ours, not like what you call your eggs. You are not his relatives. He is ours."

But the beasts disputed still. The quarrel went back and forth. And they never settled it.

The Reward for Honesty

There were four beasts living in a town, the civet, the tortoise, the antelope, and the genet. Their four houses opened on one long street. They were all neighbors.

One day in the afternoon when they all were in that street, sitting down talking, the tortoise said to them, "I have here a word to say to you."

They replied, "Well! Speak!"

At that time their town had a great famine.

The tortoise, then, said, "Tomorrow, we will go to seek food."

They replied, "Good! just as soon as the day breaks."

Then they scattered and went to their houses to lie down to sleep for the night. Soon, the day broke. And they all arose, and were ready by sunrise to go in search of food.

They searched as they walked a distance of several miles. Then they came to a plantation of Njambo's wife, Ivenga. It was about one hour's walk from Njambo's town.

The plantation had a great deal of sugar-cane, yams, and cassava. It had also some sweet potatoes. There also the chickens of Njambo often went to scratch for worms among the plants.

At once, the civet exclaimed, "I'll go no farther! I like to eat sugar-cane!"

He went, then, to the plot of cane.

The antelope also said, "I too! I'll not go any farther. I like to eat leaves of the potato and cassava."

So he went to the plot of cassava.

They were All Neighbors.

And the genet said, "Yes! I see chickens here! I like to eat chickens! I'll go no farther!"

And he went after the chickens.

But first the three had asked the tortoise, "Kudu! what will you do? Have you nothing to eat?"

The tortoise answered, "I have nothing to eat. But I shall await you even two days, and will not complain."

So the civet remarked, "Yes! I will not soon leave here, till I eat up all this cane. Then I will go back to town."

The antelope also said, "Yes! I will remain here with the potato leaves till I finish them, before I go back."

The genet also said, "Yes! I see many chickens here. I will stay and finish them."

The tortoise only said, "I have nothing to say."

In that plantation was a large tree; and the tortoise went to lie down at its foot.

They were all there four days, eating and eating. On the fifth day, Njambo's wife, Ivenga, in the town said to herself, "I'll go today, and see how my plantation is."

She came to the plantation, and when she saw the condition in which it was, she cried out and began to weep. She saw that but little cane was left, and not many potatoes. When she looked in another part of the plantation, she saw many feathers of chickens lying around. Her chickens had been killed.

She ran back rapidly to town to tell her husband, but she was so excited that she could scarcely speak. He asked her, "What's the matter, Ivenga?"

She answered, "I have no words to tell you, for the plantation is left with no food."

Then her husband called twenty men of the town, and he said to them, "Take four nets!"

They took the nets and also four dogs, with small bells tied to their necks. The men had also guns and spears and machetes in their hands. They rushed into the forest and found three of the beasts.

They came first upon the antelope and they shot him dead. Then the dogs trailed the genet and the men soon killed him. They came also upon the civet and killed him.

They took up the bodies of these beasts and said to each other, "Let us go back to town."

On the way, they came to the big tree, and found the tortoise lying by it on the ground. They took him also, and then went on their way.

When Njambo arrived there he said to the man, "Put the tortoise in a house and suspend him from the roof." He also said, "Take off the skin of the antelope and hang it in the house where the tortoise is."

He added, "Take off also the skin of the civet."

They did so, and they put it into that house. He told the man also to skin the genet and hang him up in that same house. So, there was left of these beasts in the street only the flesh of their bodies. These the men cut up and divided among themselves. And they feasted for several days.

Four days afterward Njambo said to his wife, "I'm going on a visit to a town about three miles away. While I am away, kill the tortoise and cook him with gourd seeds for me by my return."

The woman got ready the gourd seeds, and then went into the room to take the tortoise. In the dim light, she lifted up her hand and found the string to which the tortoise was hanging.

But, before she untied it, the tortoise said, "Just wait a little."

The woman took away her hand and stood waiting.

The tortoise asked her, "The skin there looks like what?"

The woman replied, "A skin of the antelope."

And the tortoise inquired, "What did the antelope do?"

The woman answered, "The antelope ate my potatoes on the plantation, and my husband killed him for it."

The tortoise said, "That is well."

Then the tortoise again asked, "This other skin is of what animal?"

The woman replied, "Of the genet."

The tortoise inquired, "What did the genet do?"

The woman answered, "The genet killed and ate our chickens, and he was killed for that."

Then the tortoise said, "Very good reason!"

Again the tortoise asked the woman, "This other skin?"

She answered, "Of the civet."

The tortoise asked, "What did the civet do?"

She answered, "The civet ate my sugar-cane, and my husband killed him."

The tortoise said, "A proper reason! But, you, you are going to kill me and cook me with gourd seed. What have I done?"

The woman had no reason to give. So she left the tortoise alive, and began to cook the gourd seeds with fish.

When Njambo came back his wife set before him the gourd seed and fish. He objected, saying, "Ah! my wife! I told you to cook the tortoise and you have cooked me fish. Why did you do this?"

The woman told him, "My husband! first finish this food, and then you and I will go to see about the tortoise."

So Njambo finished eating, and Ivenga removed the plates from the table. Then the two went into the room where the tortoise was hanging. The woman sat, but Njambo was standing ready to take down the tortoise.

Then the tortoise said to Njambo, "You, man! just wait!"

The woman also said to Njambo, "My husband! listen to what Kudu says to you."

The tortoise asked, "You, man, what skin is this?"

Njambo answered, "Of the antelope. I killed him on account of his eating my plantation."

Then the tortoise asked, "And that skin?"

Njambo answered, "Of the genet, and I killed him for eating my chickens."

The tortoise again asked, "And this other?"

Njambo answered, "Of the civet, for eating my sugarcane."

Then the tortoise said, "There were four of us on the plantation. What have I eaten? Tell me. If I have eaten of your food, then I should die."

Njambo said to him, "I've found no reason against you."

The tortoise therefore asked, "Then, why should I die?"

So Njambo untied the tortoise from the

The Tortoise goes free.

roof and said to Ivenga, "Let the tortoise go, for I find no reason against him. Let him go as he pleases."

So, Ivenga set the tortoise free. The tortoise was permitted to hasten back to his town in peace because he was not a thief. He did not eat anything on the plantation.

The Squirrel and the Spider

An industrious squirrel had labored hard to plant a crop on his farm. The farm was at last in fine condition. As the squirrel was a skillful climber of trees, he did not need to make a roadway to his farm. He used to reach it by the trees, jumping from one to the other.

One day, when the grain was very nearly ripe, it happened that the spider went out hunting nearby.

The Spider

While going along the spider arrived at the squirrel's farm.

The spider was very much pleased at the appearance of the fields, and he tried to find the road to it. As he could not find any, he came back home and told his family all about the farm.

The very next day they all started for this fine place, and

126

began at once to make a road to it. When they had made the road the spider, a very cunning fellow, built his web across it and threw pieces of earthenware along the pathway to make believe that his children had dropped them while working on the farm.

The Squirrel

Then he and his family began to cut down and carry away such of the grain as was ripe. The squirrel saw that his fields were being robbed, but could not at first find out who was doing it. He said to himself, "I will watch for the thief," and he hid himself in a tall tree nearby.

Sure enough the spider soon came again to take more of the grain. The squirrel asked the spider what right he had on his farm. The spider at once asked him the same question.

"They are my fields," said the squirrel.

"Oh, no! They are mine," replied the spider.

"I dug them and sowed them and planted them," said the poor squirrel.

"Then where is your roadway to them?" asked the crafty spider.

"I need no roadway. I come by the trees," replied the squirrel.

It is needless to say that the spider laughed at such an answer and continued to use the farm as his own.

The squirrel went to law and asked the judge to say whose farm it was; but the judge decided that no one had ever had a farm without a road leading to it; therefore the land must be the spider's.

The Spider's web across the road

In much joy the spider and his family made ready to gather all the grain that remained. When it was cut they tied it in large bundles and started for the nearest market place to sell it. When they were about halfway there, a fearful storm came up. They had to put their burdens down by the roadside and run for shelter. When

The Crow covering the grain in the road

the storm was over they returned to pick up their grain.

As they were approaching the spot they saw a large, black crow there, with his broad wings stretched over the bundles to keep them dry. The spider and his family went up to the crow and thanked him for so kindly taking care of his property, and tried to take up the bundles.

"Your property!" replied the crow. "Who ever heard of any one leaving bundles of grain by the roadside? Nonsense! This property is mine."

So saying this, he picked up the bundles and went off with them, and left the spider and his children to return home sad and empty-handed. Their thieving had done them no good. Some one had taken from them what they had taken from another.

Character

Wherever a man goes to dwell his character goes with him.

Every man's character is good in his own eyes.

Covetousness is the father of unsatisfied desires.

Disobedience is the father of insolence.

You condemn on hearsay evidence alone, your sins increase.

A man's disposition is like a mark in a stone, no one can efface it.

Gossip is unbecoming.

Charity is the father of sacrifice.

Borrowing is easy but the day of payment is hard.

He who waits for a chance may wait for a year.

You cannot kill game by looking at it.

The Toad and the Kite

The toad had lent some beads to the kite. The latter did not want to pay them back, so he kept on traveling and traveling; he was no longer seen in the village.

When the toad came to ask for the beads back again, the kite would jest; he would not even be there; he used to say:

"Tomorrow, tomorrow."

When the toad was weary to death he began to plan schemes to have a talk with the kite.

At the approach to the toad's village on this side of the river was a deserted field. It was a dry season, the grass was faded, and the toad set the field alight. When the fire was burnt out, he placed himself on a clod of earth and exposed his white stomach to the sky.

When the kite saw the smoke of the fire, he soared in the air to see whether there might not be mice lying in the fields on their backs, suffocated and dead. While he was gazing downwards, he spied something shining on a clod of earth and began to beat his wings and to say to himself, "There is a mouse."

The Toad in the home of the Kite

The kite swooped down and seized upon the
white object; he put it in his bag and carried it
through the sky; but he did not see that it was a
toad.

That evening, when he returned to his village, the kite went indoors with his mice and began to count the number in his bag. When the mice escaped, they ran, but the toad jumped out and said:

"Hulloa, Kite! Here I am. Give me my beads!"

The Toad hopping out of the Kite's bag

The kite stood amazed; he was ashamed. He proceeded to take his beads out from his secret chamber and counted them out to the toad.

"My friend, take your beads; it is right.... But how will you return to your village? I have not carried you for nothing."

The toad said, "I have taken my beads; if I had not laid a trap for you, I should not have known how to get back my loan! I know the paths which lead back to my home."

The kite did not understand the toad's cleverness. At night when he went to lie down, he hung up his bag on the door of his house very close to the ground. When the toad saw the bag, he jumped inside and remained there all night.

The kite took his bag early and went for a walk; but it became very hot, stiflingly hot. So he went to look for a river, placed his bag on the bank, and descended to the water to bathe.

The toad them jumped out, crying, "Aha, my friend! I have traveled for nothing after all!"

If the toad's limbs are feeble, his wits are not wanting.

The Antelope and the Jackal

The little antelope had been living high. He had been buying everything that was good and costly, food, drink, and the most expensive clothing. Then, as the moon rose, he would invite his friends. The drums were beating and the animals were dancing and singing till the breaking of the day drove them home; and the little antelope paid for everything.

One day after a night's feasting the little antelope awoke. He went to his money bag; but, turning it inside out and outside in, he could not find in it a single cowry to buy himself food for breakfast. He had had plenty, and now he had nothing.

"What does it matter," said the little antelope, "my friends are expecting me to continue our feasting; I will ask them to lend me some money and we shall keep on having a good time."

He found his friends at the accustomed place, but when he informed them that he wanted to borrow money they left him abruptly. Those able to run ran, those able to fly, flew. The tortoise, not able to run or to fly, drew back into its shell and shut it with a snap that sounded like a clap of thunder.

"Dear, dear," said the little antelope; "what am I to do now? My friends having treated me so shabbily. I will go to my old enemy the jackal and see what he will do for me."

Off the little antelope went and found the jackal in front of his house counting a large bag of cowries. "Hundred, hundred and one, hundred and two..."

The Antelope tells His troubles to the Jackal.

The little antelope's mouth watered at the thought of the large quantity of food this money would buy.

"Good morning, Uncle Jackal," he said humbly. "I hope you are well, and that your wife is also well, and your children too!"

"Hum," said the jackal, "hundred and ten, hundred and eleven..."

"Come another day ... hundred and twenty ... I am busy today ... hundred and twenty-one ..."

"May I come tomorrow?"

"I am going to a wedding tomorrow ... hundred and thirty ... I have to clear a field the day after ... hundred and thirty-one ... the next I have to attend a funeral ... hundred and thirty-two ... the next day..."

"The next day you will have something else to do, I have no doubt. So we might just as well do the business now. I want to ask you a little favor..."

"Ask away ... hundred and forty ... but I am afraid ... hundred and forty one ... that I won't be able to oblige you ... hundred and forty-two."

"How do you know? I have not yet told you what I want."

The jackal sneered; he had heard of the trouble his old foe was in. "I just have an idea ... hundred and fifty..."

"I want you to lend me a few cowries..."

The jackal stopped counting. "Lend you money? If you want money, why don't you go to work instead of always seeking your pleasure, you good-for-nothing scamp? Then you will get all the money you want."

"I am itching to work," said the little antelope; "work is real passion with me."

"Well, then, why don't you?"

"Did you not tell me the other day that I must never give way to my passions?"

The jackal remembered having said something like that, but somehow it did not seem to fit in just now. He wondered why. So he grumbled:

"Work ought to be a pleasure to honest people."

"Yes, yes," said the little antelope, "quite so. You have just told me that only good-for-nothing scamps always seek their pleasure."

The jackal, stupid as he was, saw now that the little antelope was making fun of him. The little antelope always did it. If only he could get his own back and play some trick on him.... Suddenly he thought of a hollow tree he had noticed the other day, and a cruel idea occurred to him.

"I will lend you no money," said he, "because, first of all, I have none; secondly, the little I own I want myself; and thirdly, what I can spare is better in my money bag than in yours. But I will help you in another way. I know of a treasure ..."

"If you know of a treasure, why don't you get it yourself?" asked the little antelope, who was on his guard.

"Because it is in a hollow tree, and, hard as I tried, I could not squeeze through the opening. You are small and slender and I will push you; you might get in."

This gave the little antelope confidence; but still he was afraid that if he did succeed in getting the treasure the jackal would take it from him as soon as he had brought it out. So he thought it might be wise to offer him beforehand a big share of it that he might be honest about the rest.

"I am willing," said he, "but as it is you who found the treasure, you must take nine-tenths of it for your share."

"No, no; keep it all," said the jackal, who could be generous—when there was nothing to lose. He well knew that there was no treasure in the hollow tree.

Then there began the strangest haggling the world has ever seen. Each one wanted to give more and to take less money as if they were in a combat. At last the little antelope, who was burning with the desire to handle the treasure, said:

"Let us agree to this: each will have an equal share, and then we shall add a little to it so that I shall have more than you and you will have more than I."

This seemed to be a fair bargain to the jackal, and he suggested that they start at once to find the treasure. Soon they came to the hollow tree. The hole was small; but the little antelope, having an empty stomach, and the jackal pushing with all his might from behind, at last got in. The antelope's tail had not yet quite disappeared, when the jackal gave a shout of joy and rolled a huge stone in front of the opening.

"Have you found anything, antelope?" asked the jackal maliciously.

"Not yet."

"I have. I have found a good dinner. Now I am going to make a big roaring fire round this tree, and when you are roasted nice and brown, you must come and have dinner with me."

"Oh, do let me out, dear jackal, do let me out!" shouted the little antelope in anguish, having found out too late that he had allowed himself to be trapped by the stupid jackal.

"Not yet, my friend. I am too busy. Look at all the wood I have to pile up to roast you."

The Antelope escapes from the Jackal.

And he went on piling up wood while the little antelope retired to the deepest recess of the hollow, trying to think of some way to escape. When the jackal had all the wood he wanted, he went to the tree and shouted!

"Halloo, antelope!" he shouted again, "are you there?"

"No," answered the little antelope.

"What!" exclaimed the jackal furiously, "how can you say that?"

"I am not telling a falsehood; I am not here."

"But are you sure of that?" asked the jackal anxiously.

"Well," giggled the little antelope, "who should know better than I? But if you doubt, take a look."

In all haste the jackal removed the twigs and then the stone; as soon a he had done so the little antelope threw some dirt into his eyes, and while the jackal was trying to remove it the little antelope slipped out of the tree. The blinded jackal soon was banging his head against the stone, against the tree, and tumbling over the twigs, while the antelope was running home as fast as he could.

Good Traits

If one knows thee not or a blind man scolds thee, do not get angry.

He who forgives ends the quarrel.

Hope is the pillar of the world.

At the bottom of patience there is heaven.

Patience is the best of qualities; he who possesses it has all things.

Property is the prop of life.

A wealthy man always has followers.

If one does good, God will interpret it to him for good.

The coming year is not out of sight, let us be up and work.

The Leopard and the Hare

Once upon a time there was some trouble between a leopard and a hare. The leopard had cheated the hare of his goat. As the leopard could not find the means to repay the hare, the leopard asked the hare to go with him to visit some kinsfolk on an island where he might obtain a goat to pay the debt.

The Leopard and the Hare on the way

The leopard said to the hare, "Make up four lunches, because the part of the lake we have to cross is dangerous, and unless you throw some food into it to appease the lake spirit you cannot cross it safely. I will also take four lunches and throw them into the lake."

The leopard, however, instead of tying up food, tied up four stones as packages and took his food in a bag. When they had floated some distance on a raft, the leopard said to the hare, "Throw over your food here."

So the hare threw his lunches into the lake.

When they reached the island, and were walking up from the shore, the leopard said, "In the bag of a great person there is always something to eat," and he took out some food and began to eat it, but he did not give the hare any.

The hare understood then that the leopard meant to starve him to death to escape paying his debt.

When they had gone a little further, the leopard said, "When the host brings us beer to drink in the place to which we are going, you go and bring a beer tube with which to drink it."

The hare promised to do so. When they arrived at the garden, they were given some beer, and the hare went to bring a beer tube, but when he came back he found the leopard had drunk all the beer.

In like manner when they were about to have a meal, the leopard said to the hare, "Go and bring a plantain stem with which we may wash our hands."

The hare went, but before he could return with it, the leopard had eaten all the food without washing his hands. The hare was very hungry, but said nothing.

In the evening after dark the leopard, unobserved, slipped out quietly, stole a little goat from the neighbors, and killed and ate it. He took some of the blood and smeared it over the head and eyebrows of the hare while he was asleep.

Early the next morning the people missed their little goat and accused the visitors of stealing it, because they traced the footprints to the house.

The leopard came out saying, "I know nothing about it, perhaps my companion does."

When the hare came out, the blood was on his head, and he was accused, tried, and condemned.

The Leopard stealing

The leopard pretended before the people that he was very angry, saying, "I will not go about with a thief; take him and kill him." The hare was then killed.

When the leopard returned home, he told a long story and pretended to be sorry for his companion who had thus been caught and killed. The brother of the hare did not believe the story. He, therefore, went to one of the spirits and asked his advice. The brother was told how the leopard had caused the death of the hare.

The brother, therefore, went to the leopard and said, "You must pay me that debt now that my brother is dead."

The leopard agreed to do so, and also expressed his sorrow for the death of the hare.

The Leopard and the Hare crossing over to the island

The leopard said, "Let us go to the island where my people live; they may help me to pay the debt."

The brother of the hare agreed, and the leopard told him he must take four lunches to appease the lake spirit.

The brother of the hare had been warned of the trick, and therefore put stones into the packages as the leopard had done; he also put two very white cowry shells and some food into his bag, and went off to meet the leopard at the lake.

When they reached the place where the leopard said the lake spirit had to be appeased, they dropped their packages into the lake, and then proceeded on the raft to the island.

When they arrived and were walking up from the lake, the leopard said, "In the bag of a great person there is always food."

The brother of the hare said, "No." He put his hand into his bag and brought out some food.

When the leopard saw this he was very angry and said, "Eat mine also; I don't like impertinent people."

When they reached the border of the garden, the leopard said, "When we come to these people and they offer us beer, you must run and bring a beer tube."

The brother of the hare thought for a moment what he could do to be even with the leopard, so he said, "I feel sick, wait while I turn aside into the grass." He had, however, gone to cut a beer tube, which he hid away in his clothing to be a match for the leopard in the next trick he would try to play.

When they reached the garden the leopard said, "When we are given food you bring a plantain stem to wash our hands."

The brother of the hare said he would, but he made an excuse to turn aside again; and while he was away he got the plantain stem and hid that also in his clothing.

When they were given beer, the leopard said, "Bring a tube for us to drink the beer."

The brother of the hare ran away, then, to get it, and came back at once with it, saying, "Do you see how quickly I run? Here is the tube."

When they were given food the leopard said, "Bring a plantain stem for us to wash our hands."

The brother of the hare ran off and came back almost at once, saying, "See how fast I run; here it is."

After sunset when they went to rest, the brother of the hare took his two cowry shells and fixed them on his eyes and went to bed. Presently the leopard slipped out quietly and stole a goat from their neighbors, which he killed and ate.

Then he brought some of the blood to put on the brother of the hare; but, seeing the white shells shining, he thought they were his open eyes and said, "Are you not asleep?"

This waked the brother of the hare and he replied, "No, I am sick."

The leopard went away for a time and then tried again, but again he found the brother of the hare apparently awake, and stole back to his bed.

By this time it was daylight and the people had missed their goat and followed the footprints to the house in which the guests were. There they called out, saying, "The visitors have stolen our goat."

The brother of the hare ran out and said, "I am no thief; examine me and see."

When the leopard came out they saw the blood on his mouth and fingers; so he was tried and condemned to death.

The brother of the hare said, "I will not go with a thief; let him be killed."

The leopard was taken and killed. The brother of the hare was thus avenged of the hare's death.

The Rabbit and the Antelope

It was during an almost rainless "hot season," when all who had no wells were beginning to feel the pangs of thirst. The rabbit and the antelope, therefore, formed a partnership to dig a deep well so that they could never be in want of water.

"Let us finish our food," said the antelope, "and be off to our work." The well must be dug at once.

Rabbit and the Antelope

"Nay," said the rabbit; "had we not better keep the food for later on, when we are tired and hungry after our work?"

"Very well, hide the food, rabbit; and let us get to work, I am very thirsty."

They arrived at the place where they purposed having the well, and worked hard for a short time.

"Listen!" said the rabbit; "they are calling me to go back to town."

"Nay, I do not hear them."

"Yes, they are certainly calling me, and I must be off. My wife is about to present me with some children, and I must name them."

150

"Go then, dear rabbit, but come back as soon as you can."

The rabbit ran off to where he had hidden the food, and ate some of it, and then went back to his work.

"Well!" said the antelope, "what have you called your little one?"

"Uncompleted one," said the rabbit.

"A strange name," said the antelope.

Then they worked for awhile.

"Again they are calling me," cried the rabbit. "I must be off, so please excuse me. Cannot you hear them calling me?"

"No," said the antelope, "I hear nothing."

Away ran the rabbit, leaving the poor antelope to do all the work, while he ate some more of the food that really belonged to them both. When he had had enough, he hid the food again, and ran back to the well.

"And what have you called your last, rabbit?"

"Half-completed one."

"What a funny little fellow you are! But come, get on with the digging; see how hard I have worked."

Then they worked hard for quite a long time. "Listen, now!" said the rabbit. "Surely you heard them calling me this time!"

"Nay, dear rabbit. I can hear nothing; but go, and get back quickly."

Away ran the rabbit, and this time he finished the food before going back to his work.

"Well, little one, what have you called your third child?"

"Completed," answered the rabbit.

Then they worked hard and as night was coming on returned to their village.

"I am terribly tired, rabbit; run and get the food, or I shall faint."

The rabbit went to look for the food, and then calling out to the antelope, told him that some horrid cat must have been there, as the food was all gone, and the pot quite clean. The antelope groaned, and went hungry to bed.

The next day the naughty little rabbit played the antelope the same trick. And the next day he again tricked the antelope. And the next, and the next, until at last the antelope accused the rabbit of stealing the food. Then the rabbit got angry, and dared him to take some medicine.

"Let us do it," said the antelope, "and let him who vomits first be considered the guilty one."

So they took the medicine. And as the medicine began to take effect upon the rabbit, he cried out to the antelope:

"See, you are vomiting first!"

"Nay, it is not!"

"Yes, it is!"

"No, it is you, dear rabbit; see there!"

Then the rabbit feared greatly, and tried to run away. But the antelope said: "Fear not, rabbit; I will do you no harm. Only you must promise not to drink of the water of my well, and to leave my company forever."

Accordingly the rabbit left him and went his way.

Some time after this, a bird told the antelope that the rabbit used to drink the water of the well every day. Then the antelope was greatly enraged, and determined to kill the rabbit. So the antelope laid a trap for the silly little rabbit. He cut a piece of wood, and shaped it into the figure of an animal about the size of the rabbit; and then he placed this figure firmly in the ground near to the well, and smeared it all over with bird lime.

The rabbit went as usual to drink the waters of the well, and was much annoyed to find an animal there, as he thought, drinking the water also.

"And what may you be doing here, sir?" said the rabbit to the figure.

The figure answered not.

Then the rabbit, thinking that it was afraid of him, went close up to it, and again asked what he was doing there.

But the figure made no answer.

"What!" said the rabbit, "do you mean to insult me? Answer me at once, or I will strike you."

The figure answered not.

Then the little rabbit lifted up his right hand, and smacked the figure in the face. His hand stuck to the figure.

"What's the matter?" said the rabbit. "Let my hand go, sir, at once, or I will hit you again."

The Rabbit caught

The figure held fast to the rabbit's right hand.
Then the rabbit hit the figure a swinging blow with
his left. The left hand stuck to the figure also.

"What can be the matter with you, sir? You are
excessively silly. Let my hands go at once, or I will
kick you."

And the rabbit kicked the figure with his right
foot; but his right foot stuck there. Then he got
into a great rage, and kicked the figure with his
left. And his left leg stuck to the figure also. Then,
overcome with rage, he bumped the figure with
his head and stomach, but these parts stuck to the
figure. Then the rabbit cried with rage.

The antelope, just about this time, came along to
drink water; and when he saw the rabbit helplessly
fastened to the figure, he laughed at him, and then
killed him.

Beware of Bad Company

The rabbit and the big snake made for themselves a big town in the ground. The ground squirrel came and said, "I want to stay with you all."

The snake replied, "All right; I agree."

But the rabbit said, "No."

The snake asked the rabbit, "Why do you not want the squirrel to stay with us?"

"Because," said the rabbit, "this ground squirrel is a rascal; he does not sit down in one place; by and by he will bring trouble on us."

"Never mind," replied the snake; "the ground squirrel shall come and stay with us; I will mind you and I will mind your little brother. What is the matter? Are you jealous of your little brother?"

Thus they lived for three months.

The rabbit remarked, "You have the power. All right; let him stay." So the rabbit went and made a little hole by himself.

155

Thus they lived for three months when the people came and made a farm near the town. Everything the people planted the squirrel would get up soon in the morning and dig up; he took up the corn, the potatoes, the cassava, and the ground nuts.

Every time the people got after the squirrel he would run to the same place. So the people decided to follow him and catch him. All the people went after the squirrel, and after digging a great deal in the ground they found him and killed him.

They said: "This squirrel is not alone. Plenty things live in this hole." So they dug on.

The rabbit whispered over to the snake: "I told you so, but this trouble is your trouble and that of your son squirrel, so I am going to my own little hiding-place."

By and by the people found the big snake and killed him. But just before he died he said, "The rabbit told me not to allow the squirrel to stay with us as he was sure to make us trouble. If you fail to take good advice, you will pay dearly for it in the end."

The people, happy for having caught the stealing squirrel and the big snake, did not dig farther, and the rabbit was safe in his little home. "Bad company is sure to lead to trouble."

The Partnership of the Elephant and the Rabbit

Once upon a time a rabbit and an elephant, coming from different ways, met on a road one day, and being old friends, stopped to greet one another, and chat about the weather and the crops, and to exchange opinions about trade. Finally the rabbit proposed that the elephant should join him in a partnership to go on a little trading trip to some shepherds, "Because," said he, "I hear there are some good chances to make profit among them. Cloth, I am told, is very scarce there, and I think we might find a good bargain awaiting us."

The elephant was delighted and accepted the offer of his little friend. Two bales of goods were prepared for the journey.

They set out on good terms with each other, and the rabbit, with his many experiences, amused the elephant greatly. By and by the friends arrived at a river, and the elephant, to whom the water was agreeable, stepped in to cross it, but halted on hearing the rabbit exclaim:

"Why, elephant, you surely are not going to cross without me? Are we not partners?"

"Of course we are partners, but I did not agree to carry you or your pack. Why don't you step right in? The water is not deep, it scarcely covers my feet."

"But, you stupid fellow," said the rabbit, "can you not see that what will scarcely cover your feet is more than enough to drown me, and I can't swim a bit; and, besides, if I get my fur wet I shall catch the ague, and how ever am I to carry my pack across?"

"Well, I cannot help that," replied the elephant. "It was you who proposed to take the journey, and I thought a wise fellow like you would have known that there were rivers running across the road, and that you knew what to do. If you cannot travel, then good-by. I cannot stop here all day," and the elephant walked on across to the other side.

"Surly rascal," muttered the rabbit. "All right, my big friend, I will pay you for it some time."

Not far off, however, the rabbit found a log, and after placing his pack on it, he paddled himself over, and reached the other bank safely; but to his grief he found out that his bale had been wetted and damaged.

The rabbit wiped the water off as much as possible, and resumed the journey with the elephant, which had looked carelessly on the efforts of his friend to cross the river.

Fortunately for the rabbit, there were no more wide streams to be crossed. The journey did not present such difficulties, and they arrived in due time among the shepherds.

Now at a trade the elephant was not to be compared with the rabbit, for he could not talk so pleasantly as the rabbit, and he was not at all sociable. The rabbit went among the women, and laughed and joked with them, and said so many funny things, that they were delighted with him, and when at last the question came up, a chief's wife was so kind to him that she gave a mighty fine cow in exchange for his little bale of cloth.

The elephant, in the meantime, went among the men, and simply told them that he had come to buy cattle with cloth. The shepherds did not like his appearance or his manner, and said they had no cattle to sell, but if he cared to have it, they would give a year-old heifer for his bale. Though the elephant's bale was a very heavy one, and many times more valuable than the rabbit's, yet as he was so gruff and ugly, he was at last obliged to be satisfied with the little heifer.

Just as they had left the shepherds to return home, the elephant said to the rabbit, "Now mind, should we meet any one on the road, and be asked whose cattle these are, I wish you to oblige me by saying that they are mine, because I should not like people to believe that I am not as good a trader as you are. They will also be afraid to touch them if they know they belong to me; but if they hear they belong to you, every fellow will think he has as good a right to them as you have, and you dare not protect your property."

"Very well," replied the rabbit, "I quite understand."

In a little while, as the rabbit and the elephant drove their cattle along, they met many people coming from market, who stopped and admired them, and said, "Ah, what a fine cow is that! to whom does it belong?"

"It belongs to me," answered the thin voice of the rabbit. "The little one belongs to that big elephant."

"Very fine indeed. A good cow that," replied the people, and passed on.

Vexed and annoyed, the elephant cried angrily to the rabbit, "Why did you not answer as I told you? Now mind, do as I tell you at the next meeting with strangers."

"Very well," answered the rabbit, "I will try and remember."

By and by they met another party going home with fowls and palm wine, who, when they came up, said, "Ah, that is a fine beast, and in prime order. Whose is it?"

"It is mine," quickly replied the rabbit, "and the little scabby heifer belongs to the elephant."

The answer enraged the elephant, who said, "What an obstinate little dunce you are! Did you not hear me ask you to say it was mine? Now, remember, you are to say so next time, or I leave you to find your own way home, because I know you are a horrible little coward."

"Very well, I'll try to think of it next time," replied the rabbit in a meek voice.

In a short time they met another crowd of people who stopped when opposite to them and said, "Really, that is an exceedingly fine cow. To which of you does it belong?"

"It is mine. I bought it from the shepherds," replied the rabbit.

The elephant was so angry this time that he broke away from the rabbit and drove his little heifer by another road. To the animals in the forest he remarked that a fine fat cow was being driven by the cowardly little rabbit along the other road. He did this out of mere spite, hoping that some one

Giving away the Secret

of them would be tempted to take it by force from the rabbit.

But the rabbit was wise. He had seen the spite in the elephant's face as he went off, and was sure that he would play him some unkind trick; and, as night was falling and his home was far, and he knew that there were many vagabonds lying in wait to rob poor travelers, the rabbit knew that if his wit failed to save him he would be in great danger.

True enough, it was not long before a big bluster-ing lion rose from the side of the road, and cried out, "Hello, you there. Where are you going with that cow? Come, speak out."

"Ah, is that you, lion?" said the rabbit. "I am tak-ing it to Mugassa (the deity), who is about to give a feast to all his friends, and he told me particularly to invite you to share it, if I should meet you."

"Eh? What? To Mugassa?" inquired the lion. "Oh, well, I am proud to have met you, rabbit. As I am not otherwise engaged I will accompany you, because every one considers it an honor to wait upon Mugassa."

They proceeded a little further, and a bouncing buffalo came up and bellowed fiercely, "You, rabbit, stop," said he. "Where are you taking that cow?"

"I am taking it to Mugassa, don't you know? How would a little fellow like me have the courage to go so far from home if it were not that I am in the service of Mugassa? I am charged also to tell you, buffalo, that if you like to join in the feast Mugassa

Where are you going with that Cow?

is about to give, he will be glad to have you as a guest."

"Oh, well, that is good news indeed," said the buffalo. "I will come along now, rabbit, and am very glad to have met you. How do you do, lion?"

A short distance off the party met a huge rogue elephant, which stood in the middle of the road, and in a tone which required a quick answer, demanded to know where the cow was being taken.

"Now, elephant, get out of the way," said the rabbit. "This cow is being taken to Mugassa, who will be angry with you if I am delayed. Have you not heard of the feast he is about to give? By the bye, as you are one of the guests, you might as well help me to drive this cow, and let me get on your back, for I am dreadfully tired."

"Why, that's grand," said the elephant. "I shall be delighted to feast with Mugassa, and—come, get on my back. I will carry you with pleasure. And, rabbit," whispered the elephant, as he lifted him by his trunk, "don't forget to speak a good word for me to Mugassa."

All going along to the feast

Soon a leopard and then a hyena were met, but seeing such a powerful crowd behind the cow, they became very calm, and were invited to accompany the rabbit's party to Mugassa's feast.

It was quite dark by the time they arrived at the rabbit's village. At the gate stood two dogs which were the rabbit's chums, and they barked furiously; but hearing their friend's voice, they came up and welcomed the rabbit.

The party halted, and the rabbit, after reaching the ground, whispered to the dogs how affairs stood, and the dogs wagged their tails approvingly, and yauped with fun as they heard of the rabbit's wit. It did not take long for the dogs to understand what was required of them, and one of them returned with a pretended message from the great Mugassa.

"Well, my friends, do you hear what Mugassa says?" cried the rabbit, with a voice of importance.

"The dogs are to lay mats inside the village by the gate, and the cow is to be killed, and the meat prepared nicely and laid on the mats. And when this is done, Mugassa himself will come and give each his portion. He says that you are all very welcome.

"Now listen to me before I go in to Mugassa, and I will show you how you can all help to hurry the feast, for I am sure you are all anxious to begin.

"You, hyena, must kill the cow, and dress the meat and the dogs will carry it in and lay it on the mats; but remember, if a bit is touched before Mugassa commands, we are all ruined.

"You, elephant, must take this brass hatchet of Mugassa's, and split wood nicely for the hearth.

"Buffalo, go and find a wood with a smooth bark, which burns well, and bring it to the elephant.

"Leopard, go to the banana plantation, and watch for the falling leaf and catch it with your eyelids, in order that we may have proper plates.

"Lion, my friend, go and fill this pot from the spring, and bring water that Mugassa may wash his hands."

Having issued his instructions, rabbit went strutting into the village; but after he had gone a little way he darted aside, and passing through a side door, went out and crept toward an ant hill. On the top was a tuft of grass, and from his hiding-place he commanded a view of the gate, and of all who might come near it.

Now the buffalo could find only one log with smooth bark, and the dogs shouted out to the buffalo that one log was not enough to roast or to boil the meat, and he returned to hunt up some more.

The elephant struck the log with his brass hatchet, which was broken at the first blow, and there was nothing else with which to cut the wood.

The leopard watched and watched for falling leaves but failed to see any.

The lion's pot had a hole in the bottom, and he could never keep it full, though he tried ever so many times.

Meanwhile, the hyena having killed the cow and dressed the meat beautifully, said to the dogs, "Now, my friends, the meat is ready. What shall I do?"

"You can help us carry the meat in, and lay it on the mats, if you like, for Mugassa must see it before anybody can touch it."

"Ah, but I feel extremely hungry, and my mouth waters so that I am sick with longing. May we not go shares and eat a little bit? It looks very nice and fat," whined the hyena.

"Ah, no, we should not dare do such a thing. We have long ago left the woods, and its habits, and are unfit for anything but human society; but if you were allowed to eat any, you could fly into the woods, and we should have all the blame. No, no, come, help us carry it inside. You will not have to wait long."

The hyena was obliged to obey, but contrived to hide in the grass some of the tripe. The rabbit, from behind his tuft of grass, saw it all, and winked in the dark.

When the meat was in, the dogs said, "It is all right now. Just stay outside until the other fellows arrive."

The hyena retired, and when he was outside of the gate searched for his tripe, and lay down quietly to enjoy it, but as he was about to bite it, the rabbit screamed, "Ah, you thief, hyena. You thief, I see you. Stop, thief, Mugassa is coming!"

These cries so alarmed the hyena that he dropped his tripe, and fled away as fast as his legs could carry him, and the others, the buffalo, elephant, lion, and leopard, tired out with waiting, and hearing these alarming cries, also ran away, leaving the rabbit and his dog friends in quiet possession. They carried the tripe into the village, and closed the gate and barred it, after which they laughed loud and long, the rabbit rolling on the ground over and over with the fun of it all.

The rabbit was the smallest of all, but by his wisdom he was more than a match for two elephants, the buffalo, the leopard, the lion, the hyena, and all. And even his friends, the dogs, had to confess that the rabbit's wit could not be matched.

Thoughts of Africans

There are three friends in this world—courage, sense, and insight.

A person prepared beforehand is better than after reflection.

The day on which one starts is not the time to commence one's preparation.

Lack of knowledge is darker than night.

An ignorant man is always a slave.

Whoever works without knowledge works uselessly.

Trade is not something imaginary or descriptive, but something real and profitable.

Three Rival Brothers

Three brothers took a walk. They stopped at a town and fell in love with the king's daughter, and each wanted to marry her.

The king told them that he would give her to the one who brought him a servant. So they started out in search of a servant and traveled many days into strange lands.

Each one of the brothers had something with which he could do wonders. One of the brothers had a glass into which he could look and find out each day everything that had happened in the town he had passed. One of the others had a hammock into which one might sit, and be carried anywhere he wished to go. The third brother had some medicine with which he could raise the dead if they had not been dead more than three days.

After they had walked two weeks in search of a servant one morning the brother with the glass looked into it and found out that the king's daughter was dead, and that she had died on the third day before. He told the other brothers the sad news.

The brother with the medicine said that he could restore her to life if he could reach the town on that very day, before the third day had ended, but that they were more than two weeks' walk to the town.

The other brother said:

"That is all right. Come, get into my hammock."

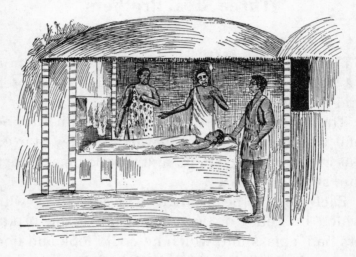

Three Rivals standing over the dead Daughter

They all sat down and in a few moments they were in the town.

They went to the king and asked what was the news.

"Nothing," said the king, "except that my daughter you all love is dead, having died three days ago today."

The brother with the medicine asked the king what he would give him, if he restored his daughter to life? The king promised him the daughter and all his wealth. The daughter was immediately raised from the dead with the medicine, and the brother who had the medicine claimed the daughter.

The brother who had the glass claimed her because, as he said, "But for my finding out that she was dead we would not have known that she was dead in time to restore her."

"She belongs to me," said the brother with the hammock, "for although you knew she was dead we were two weeks' walk away, and but for my hammock we could never have reached here with your medicine before the third day closed."

The Judge walked away.

Unable to agree, the brothers began to disturb the peace. The people came and tried to persuade them to settle the trouble quietly but they refused to listen to their advice. The whole matter was then taken to the judge. After patiently listening to what the father and three brothers had to say, the judge was unable to decide the case. He turned it over to the people and walked away saying, "This question is too difficult for me." The people were never able to decide the case.

To which one of the brothers did the daughter belong?

The Legend of Ngurangurane

There was in the olden times—it is a long time since that, quite a long time—a very great magician, and it was Ngurangurane, the son of the Crocodile.

And here is how he was born, that is the first thing: what he did and how he died, that is the second. To tell all his actions it is impossible, and, besides, who would remember them?

Here is how he was born, that is the first thing.

At that time, the Fangs were living on the bank of a large river, large, so large that one could not see the other side; they used to fish from the border. But they did not go on the river; no one yet had taught them how to build canoes: he who taught it to them, it was Ngurangurane. Ngurangurane taught this art to the men of his family, and, his family, they were the men, they were the Fangs.

In the river lived an enormous crocodile, the master crocodile; his head was longer than this cabin, his eyes were bigger than a whole kid, his teeth could cut a man in two as one cuts a banana. He was covered with enormous scales: a man could strike him with his javelins, too, but, *pfat*, the

172

javelin fell back; and he who did thus he could be the most robust man: *pfut*, the javelin fell back. It was a terrible animal.

Now, one day, he came into the village of Ngurangurane; but this one was not yet born. And the one who was commanding the Fangs was a great chief, and he commanded many men. He commanded the Fangs and others besides. Ngan Esa, the master crocodile, came then one day into the village of the Fangs and he called the chief: "Chief, I call you."

The chief hastened at once. And the crocodile chief said to the man chief: "Listen attentively."

And the man chief answered: "Ears" (that is to say, I listen well).

The Crocodile calls for toll.

"What you shall do from today on, this is it. Each day I am hungry, and I think that the flesh of the man is better for me than the flesh of the fish. Each day, you shall bind a slave and you shall bring it for me on the bank of the river, a man one day, a woman the next day, and, on the first day of each moon, a young girl well painted with baza and all shining with grease. You shall do thus. If you dare to disobey me, I shall eat your whole village. There! This is ended. Speak not."

And the crocodile chief, without adding a word, returned to the river. And in the village, they began mournful lamentations. And each one said: "I am dead." Each one said it, the chief, the men, the women. The next day, in the morning, when the sun rose, the crocodile chief was on the bank of the river. "Wah! Wah!" his mouth was enormous, longer than this cabin, his eyes were large like a whole kid. The crocodiles that you see today are not crocodiles any more! And they hastened to bring to the crocodile chief that which he had asked, a man one day, a woman the next day and, on the first day of each moon, a young girl painted with red and all shining with grease. They did that which the crocodile chief had ordered, and none dared disobey, for he had everywhere his warriors, the other crocodiles.

And the name of this crocodile, it was Ombure: the waters were obeying Ombure, the forests were obeying Ombure, his "men" were everywhere, he was master of the forest, but he was above all master of the water. And, each day, he ate either a man, or a woman, and he was very pleased and very friendly to the Fangs. But these, finally, had given all their slaves and, to buy some, the chief had handed over all his riches. He had not one coffer left, not one elephant tooth! He had to give a man, a Fang man! And the chief of the Fangs gathered all his people in the common cabin; he spoke to them a long, long time, and after him the other warriors spoke also a long time. When the conference was ended, every one agreed and thought with one heart that they should depart. The chief then said: "Now this question of departure is settled: we shall go far, far from here, beyond the mountains. When we shall be far, very far from the river, beyond the mountains, Ombure will not be able to reach us, and we shall be happy."

And it was decided that they would not renew the plantings, and that at the end of the season the whole tribe would leave the banks of the river. And thus it was done.

Carried away by the Crocodile

At the beginning of the dry season, when the waters are low, and traveling is good, the tribe started to march. The first day, they went quickly, quickly, as quickly as they could. Each man hurried his women, and the women, quickening their pace, marched in silence, bending under the load of the provisions and the household utensils, because they were carrying away everything, pots, dishes, pestles, baskets, swords and hoes, everything; each woman had her load and she had it heavy. She had it heavy because, with all that, they had also dried some manioc and carried it away. She had it heavy, because she had also to carry the children, the little ones who could not walk and those who were beginning to walk.

And they had to be silent: the men were silent, the women were silent, and the children were crying, but the mothers said: "Be quiet." The great chief was at the head: he led the march, for it was he who knew the country the best: he often had been hunting, and around his neck he wore a necklace of a big monkey's teeth.

He was indeed a great hunter.

On the first day, many looked behind them, they thought they heard the crocodile: Wah! Wah! And he who was at the end felt cold in his heart! But they heard nothing. And on the second day, the march was the same, and they heard nothing. And on the third day, the march was the same, and they heard nothing.

On the first day, however, the crocodile chief had come out of the water, according to his habit, in order to come to the place where he used to find the slave who had been destined for him. He comes: "Wah! Wah!" Nothing. What is this? He takes at once the road to the village.

"Chief of the men, I call you."

Nothing! He hears no noise; he enters; all the cabins are abandoned: "Wah! Wah!" he goes through all the villages, all the villages are abandoned; he goes through all the plantations, all the plantations are abandoned.

Ombure then flies into a terrible rage and dives again into the river to consult his fetish, and he sings:

You who command to the waters, spirits of the waters,
All you who obey me, it is I who call to you,
Come, come to the call of your master,
Answer without delay, answer immediately.
I shall send the lightning which flashes through the sky,
I shall send the thunder which breaks all on his path,
I shall send the wind of the tempest that tears down the banana trees.
I shall send the storm which falls from the clouds and sweeps everything in front of him.
And all will answer to the voice of their master.
All you who obey me, show me the road,
The road which those who have fled have taken.
Spirits of the waters, answer.

But to his great surprise, the spirits of the waters do not answer, not a single one answers!

What then had happened? This. Before leaving his village, the chief of the men had offered great sacrifices. He had offered a great sacrifice to the spirits of the waters, asking them to remain mute and they had promised. They had promised: "We will say nothing."

Ombure begins again a conjuration, a stronger one still:

You who command to the waters, spirits of the waters,
All you who obey me, it is I who call you....

And the spirits of the waters, forced to obey, appear before Ombure:

"Where are the men, have they used your roads?" "We have seen nothing, they have not used our roads," (And Ombure says: "They have not used the roads of the waters: the spirits of the waters could not disobey me.")

And he calls the spirits of the forests:

You who command to the forests, spirits of the forests,
All you who obey me, it is I who call to you,
Come, come to the call of your master,
Answer without delay, answer immediately.
I shall send the lightning that flashes through the sky.
I shall send the thunder which breaks all on his path,
I shall send the wind of the tempest which tears down the
*   banana trees,*
I shall send the storm which falls from the clouds and
*   sweeps everything in front of him.*
And all will answer to the voice of their master.
All you who obey me, show me the road,
The road which those who have fled have taken,
Spirits of the forests, answer.

But, to his great surprise, of all the spirits of the forests, not one spirit answers, all are silent.

What then had happened? This. Before leaving his village, the chief of the men had offered great sacrifice to the spirits of the forests, asking them to remain mute, and they had promised: "We will say nothing."

Ombure began again a conjuration, a stronger one still:

You who command to the forests, spirits of the forests,
All you who obey me, it is I who call you.

And the spirits of the forests, forced to obey,
appear before Ombure. "Where are the men, have
they passed through your roads?"

And the spirits of the forests answer: "They have
not passed through our roads."

And, successively, Ombure calls the spirits of the
day, the spirits of the night, and, thanks to them,
he knows the road which the Fangs have taken.

They have told him the news!

And when Ombure had ended his enchantment,
he knew the road which the fugitive Fangs had
taken. These had concealed their path in vain. Ombure knew their road. Who had told it to him? The
lightning, the wind, the storm had told it to him;
the lightning, the wind and the storm.

The Fangs continued their march for a long time,
a very long time. They crossed the mountains, and
the great chief consulted his fetish:

"Shall we stop here?"

And the fetish, who, since a long time, since the
first day, was obeying the orders of Ombure (but this
the chief did not know), the fetish answered, "No,
you shall not stop here, this is not a good place."

They crossed the plains, and when they had
crossed the plains and had found again the great
forest, the forest that never ends, the great chief
consulted his fetish, "Shall we stop here?"

And the fetish, once more, answered, "Further yet."

They arrived finally in a great plain, in front of a great lake which closed all passage, and the great chief consulted his fetish, "Shall we stop here?"

And the fetish who obeyed Ombure answered, "Yes, you shall stop here."

And the Fangs had walked many days and many moons. The little children had become youths, the youths had become young warriors and the young warriors, matured men. They had walked many days and many moons. They stopped on the banks of the lake. They built new villages, plantings were made and everywhere the corn gave its new yield. The chief then gathered his men in order to give a name to the village, and they called it Akurengan (Deliverance-from-the Crocodile).

But, that very night, toward midnight, a great noise is heard and a voice cries, "Oh! come, come here." And all go out, very scared. What do they see? (The moon was very bright.) Ombure was in the middle of the village. He was in front of the great chief's cabin. What is to be done? Where to can one run? Where can one hide? No one dared to think about it! And when the great chief came out to see what was happening, "Yu," he was the first one to be taken! With a single bite, Ombure cut him in two! "Kro, Kro, Kwas!" —"There! Akurengan," he said.

And he returned toward the lake.

The trembling warriors chose at once another chief, the brother of the last one, according to the law; and, in the morning, they took the wife of the last chief and they bound her on the bank of the lake, as an offering to Ombure. And he came; the woman was crying. Kro, Kro! he ate her. But, in the evening, he came back to the village and called the chief:

"Chief, I call you."

And this one, trembling, answered, "I listen."

"This is what I command to you, I, Ombure, and you shall do it. Every day, you shall bring two men, one man in the morning, one man in the evening, and the next day, you shall bring me two women, one woman in the morning and one woman in the evening. And on the first day of each moon, two young girls painted with red and shining with oil. Go, this is I, Ombure, the king of the forest; this is I, Ombure, the king of the waters."

And thus they did during many years. Each morning, each evening, Ombure had his meal: two men one day, two women the next day and two young girls on the first day of the month. Thus it happened for a long time. In order to pay Ombure, the Fangs made war far, far away. And everywhere they were the victors, because Ombure, the crocodile chief, protected them, and they became great warriors.

But the years passed, one after the other, and for a long time the Fangs had renewed their plantings. And they were tired of Ombure.

And they had forgotten. And the young men said: "We are tired, let us leave." And the young men left in front, the warriors followed, and the women carried the bundles after the warriors.

The Crocodile in the village

The next morning Ombure came on the bank of the lake to seek his daily food, as was his habit. He looks, he searches. Nothing. He comes to the village. Nothing. What does he do? He takes his fetish and calls at once the spirits of the forest.

"This is what commands to you, Ombure, your master," he says to them: "My slaves have fled, they are in your domain, let all passages close in front of them. Wind of the storm, break the trees in front of them; spirit of the thunder, spirit of the lightning, blind their eyes! Go, it is Ombure who commands you."

And they go. The roads close in front of the Fangs, the big trees fall, darkness invades everything. In despair, they have to return to the lake, and there Ombure awaits them. But Ombure is old; instead of two men, he now demands, "You shall give me each day two young girls as a sacrifice."

And the Fangs had to obey and each day had to bring two young girls to Ombure, two young girls painted with red and shining and rubbed with oil. It is their wedding festival.

They cry and mourn, the daughters of the Fangs; they cry and mourn; it is the festival of the sad betrothing.

They cry and mourn in the evening; in the morning, they do not cry nor do they mourn: their mothers do not hear from them any more: they are at the bottom of the lake, in the grotto where Ombure lives. They serve him, and he makes his food of them.

But one day, there happened this: The young girl who had to be taken to the bank of the river that evening; the young girl whose turn had come, it was Alena-Kiri, the child of the chief. She was young and she was beautiful. And, in the evening, she was bound on the bank of the lake, with her companion. The companion did not return, but the next day, when daylight appeared again, the chief's daughter was still there. Ombure had spared her.

Therefore they called her: "Dawn has come."

But nine months later, the chief's daughter had a child, she had a son. In remembrance of his birth, this boy was named Ngurangurane, the son of the crocodile.

Ngurangurane was then the Son of Ombure, the crocodile chief: this is the first story. Ngurangurane was thus born.

Here is the second story: the death of Ombure.

Ngurangurane, the child of the crocodile Ombure and the chief's daughter, grew, grew, grew, each day. From a child, he became a youth, from a youth he became a young man. He is then the chief of his people. He is a powerful chief and a very learned magician. In his heart he had two desires: to avenge the death of the chief of his race, his mother's father, and to free his people from the tribute which the crocodile exacted.

To attain this end, here is what he did:

In the forest there is a sacred tree, this you know; and this tree they call it "palm tree." Cut a palm tree: the sap flows, flows abundantly, and if you wait two or three days, after having enclosed it in earthen vessels, you will have the dzan, the drink that makes the heart happy. This, we know it now, but our fathers did not know it. He taught it to them, it was Ngurangurane, and the first one who drank the dzan it is Ombure, the crocodile chief. Who taught Ngurangurane about the dzan? It was Ngonomane, the fetish stone which his mother had given him.

Now, following Ngonomane's advice, Ngurangurane did thus:

"Take all the earthen vessels that you possess, all of them, bring them into my cabin."

He said that to the women: they brought then all the earthen vessels they possessed, and there were many and many of them.

"Go, all, into the forest," he said to them again, "near the brook with the clay and make more vessels yet."

And they went to the brook with the clay and made some vessels, many of them.

"Let us go into the forest," he said to the men. "Let us go and you will cut the trees that I shall show to you."

And they went, all together, with hatchets and with knives, and they cut the trees which Ngurangurane showed them. These trees, they were palm trees. And when they were all cut, they collected the sap which was flowing abundantly from the wounds. The vessels were brought (the women did that), the old vessels and the new ones, and when all were there they filled them with the dzan, and the women carried them back to the village. Every day, Ngurangurane tasted the liquor; the men wanted to do like him, but this he forbid them by a great eki.

A man said, "Since Ngurangurane drinks of it, I shall drink of it."

And he drank of it, but in secret, and it went to his head. Ngurangurane came near him and killed him with a gun shot.

Three days later, Ngurangurane gathered his men, the men and the women, and said to them:

"This is the time, take the vessels and come with me to the bank, near the lake." They took the vessels and went with him. When they were on the bank of the lake, Ngurangurane ordered this to his men: "Bring on the bank all the vessels." And they did it. "Bring the clay for which I sent you," he said to the women, and thus they did. And, on the bank of the lake, with the soft clay they built two large basins, carefully beaten with the feet, carefully smoothed with the palm of the hands. Then, into the two basins they pour all the dzan that was contained in the vessels, without leaving one drop; Ngurangurane begins a great fetish, and they break then all the vessels, and they throw them into the lake. They bind the two captives near the basins and every one goes back to the village.

Ngurangurane stays alone, hidden near the basins.

At the usual hour, the crocodile comes out of the water. He goes toward the captives who were trembling with fear; but, first of all:

"What is this?" he says as he comes near the basins. "What is this?"

He tastes a little of the liquid. The liquor seems good to him and he cries aloud: "This is good; from tomorrow on I shall order the Fangs to give me some of it every day."

And Ombure, the crocodile, drank the dzan. He drank it to the last drop, forgetting the captives. When he had finished, he sang:

*I have drunk the dzan, the liquor which brings joy to the
  heart:*
I have drunk the dzan,
I have drunk the dzan, my heart is rejoicing,
I have drunk the dzan.
The master whom all obey, it is I,
I, the great chief, I, Ombure.
It is I, Ngan, I am the master.
Ombure is master of the waters,
Ombure is master of the forests.
It is I, the master whom all obey.
I am the master.
*I have drunk the dzan, the liquor which brings joy to the
  heart;*
I have drunk the dzan.
I have drunk the dzan, my heart rejoices;
I have drunk the dzan.

He sings, and on the sand, forgetting the captives, he falls asleep, joy in his heart.

Ngurangurane at once comes near Ombure asleep; with a strong rope, and helped by the captives, he binds him to the post, then brandishing with force his javelin, he strikes the sleeping animal; on the thick scales, the javelin bounces back without touching the crocodile, and this one, still asleep, shakes himself and says: "What is this? a mosquito has bitten me."

Ngurangurane takes his hatchet, his strong stone hatchet; with an immense blow he strikes the sleeping animal: the hatchet bounces back without wounding the animal; this one begins to move: the two captives, terrified, run away. Ngurangurane makes then a powerful fetish: "Thunder," he says, "thunder, it is you whom I call, bring me your arrows."

And the lightning came. But when he learns that he must kill Ombure: "It is your father," he cries, "and it is my master." And, frightened, he went away. But Alena Kiri comes to help her son, and she brings Ngonomane, the fetish stone. And in the name of Ngonomane, Ngurangurane says: "Lightning, I command you to strike."

And the lightning strikes, for he could not disobey. On the head, between the eyes, he strikes Ombure, and Ombure remains immobile, thunderstruck, dead. He who has killed him, it is Ngurangurane, but Ngurangurane killed him with the help of Ngonomane.

And the end of this story, here it is:

Ngurangurane hastens back to the village. "All you, men of the village," he says, "all you, come," and they all came on the bank of the lake. Ombure is there, lying dead, immense. "He who has killed Ombure, the crocodile, it is I, Ngurangurane. He who has avenged the chief of his race, it is I; he who has freed you, it is I, Ngurangurane."

All rejoiced and, around the corpse, they danced the fanki, the great funeral dance; they danced the fanki for the spirit of Ombure must be appeased.

And this is the end of Ombure.

Self-pronouncing Words

The vowels are pronounced very much as they are in Latin.

A-fī'-ong
A-ku-ren'-gan
A-le'-na-Ki-ri
A-nan'-si
An'-sa
A-wi-re'-hu
Bo'-a
Can-e-tie-tie
D'zan
E'-dem
Ef'-fī-ong
E'-Jimm
Fangs
Gu-lu'
Ig'-we
I-san-tim
I-ven'-ga
Kai-ku'-zī
Kâ-kâ-re'-kââ
Kin-tu'
Ko-do'-ko
Kro Kro
Ku-du
K'we-ku
K'we'-ku-Tsin

Lu-em'-ba
Ma-vun'gu (u like oo in noon)
Ma-vu-ng-u-a-a-a
Mbru-kâ-kâ
Mu-gas'-sa
Mu-zi'-mu
Nam-bĭ'
N'gan-e-sa
N'go-no'-ma-ne'
N'gu-ran-gu-ra-ne
N'jam'-bi
N'j-am'-bo
N'tun
O-băs-si
O-bas'-si
O-be'-gud
O-du-dua'
O-hi'-a
O-kŭn'
O-lo-run
Om'-bu-re
O'rī'-sha
Wah-wah
Wa-ka-san'-ke
Wa-lum'-bē